**Other Books by Evelyn Allen Harper**

*The Coat*
*The Collar*
*Sweet Adeline*
*The Tale of the Unread Book*
*Decisions*

The Accidental Mystery Series

*And So To Sleep*
*And So To Dream*
*The Wrath of Grapes*
*And So To Love*
*And So it Goes*
*The Wrath of Winter*

# Essence

By Evelyn Allen Harper

Ink Smith Publishing

www.ink-smith.com

ISBN: 978-1-939156-98-3

Ink Smith Publishing
710 S. Myrtle Ave Suite 209
Monrovia, CA, 91016

# Chapter 1

Laura Baker sighed, laid her book down, and waved off the waitress who was approaching her table with a coffee carafe in her hand. Laura felt guilty about tying up the table for an hour but when the crushing stillness of her house had become unbearable, she'd grabbed a book and her car keys, and fled.

With both kids off at camp, a husband who worked long hours, and a close friend who was seldom available, the long days were getting to her. The announcement that Ben had made nine years ago as they waited for the pregnancy stick to change color had sounded romantic at the time, but it didn't sound romantic anymore. Lately, his statement, "The mother of my children will never work outside the home," felt like a prison sentence. Her pathetic need to be in a social setting just to hear voices and see activity had sent her to a coffee shop to read, while pretending to be waiting for a friend.

The waitress was smiling when she asked, "Book boring or did you get stood up?"

Laura made up a story. "Both," she grinned. "My friend always has such interesting excuses, but this one better be good!"

While leaning down to pick up her purse, she was surprised when she recognized a very familiar sound. Even after two children and ten years of marriage, just hearing her husband's deep voice still had the power to excite her. The hostess was seating him at a nearby table, which was silly because she already had a perfectly good table to share with him. With a girlish giggle, she was about to call out a greeting when the sound of a second voice, a very familiar female one, stopped her. Laura kept her head down.

With disbelieving eyes, she watched her handsome husband hold the chair for a tall slim blond who was looking up at him with adoring eyes. Like a bad dream, she watched Ben lean down, cup the woman's face with his hands and passionately kiss Joan, her best friend.

Stunned beyond belief, she remained frozen in her position, feeling bewildered, humiliated, and betrayed. Her first thought was to run, but the only way out would take her by their table.

"Is there something wrong?"

Startled, Laura looked up to find the waitress with the coffee carafe was back. Struggling to talk over the lump in her throat, she replied, "Yes, there is. I need to get out of here without being seen."

When the waitress raised her eyebrows, Laura nodded her head in the direction of her husband's table. The waitress took one look at the entwined couple and said, "Follow me."

Pointing at a door, she added, "That will take you to the kitchen, and there's a door in the back that exits to the parking lot."

The bitter taste of coffee that was making its way up her throat put speed into her trip through the kitchen. Trying to shut out the greasy smells, she made it outside to a bush before her stomach revolted.

Ben and her best friend? How could that be? And why would Joan do that to her? Ben's long hours at work and Joan's lack of availability were now making sense. How long had this been going on? Her picture-perfect marriage with a white picket fence, two kids, and a shaggy dog was a lie. It almost shocked her when she discovered that losing her best friend was almost as painful as losing Ben.

# Chapter 2

The absolute silence that surrounded her the moment she stepped into the house was suffocating. Breaking the quiet was the welcoming sound of Roscoe's claws clicking on the hardwood floor. The big shaggy dog, who dropped enough fur in a day to knit a sweater, was wagging his tail in anticipation of a trip outside.

Laura knelt down and buried her face in his fur. "Roscoe," she sobbed. "What do I do now?" Sensing that something was wrong, he licked the tears that were running down her cheeks.

"Good old dog," she whispered.

Noticing that he was now dancing in place, she opened the door. "Go be a good boy!" she called after him as he ran out into the fenced-in yard. Alone again, she leaned against the door and slid silently to the floor. Feeling utterly devastated, she placed her elbows on her knees, covered her face with her hands, and while tears flowed down from between her fingers, she cried. "Joan, Joan, how could you do this to me?" A ping from her cell phone broke into her misery. Picking it up, she saw it was a text from Ben.

> Ben: *Working overtime again. Don't bother cooking dinner for me. The boss is feeding us. Love u*

Slowly she pushed herself off the floor and opened the door for Roscoe who rushed in looking for a treat.

Coffee. Automatically her hands went through the routine of setting up her coffee maker while her mind was elsewhere. Anger was building up inside her for the injustice of the whole situation. Being a good wife, she had obeyed her husband and never went back to work after their first child was born. Her two university degrees went unused because of Ben's decree. So maybe she had become boring. So maybe she had taken Ben for granted. So maybe....

By the second cup of coffee she had managed to assess the situation. For now, she had the upper hand. Joan's husband, John, had a job that involved a lot of traveling. That could mean that right now he was out of town and after lunch the two lovebirds would go to Joan's house.

Laura cleaned the kitchen, giving them time to finish lunch and get comfortable at Joan's house before she picked up her cell and texted.

Laura: *Haven't seen you in ages. Right now I'm in your neighborhood. See you in a few.*

She waited until the word delivered appeared under her sent text before she allowed herself to breathe.

Her cell pinged.

Joan: *Oh, no! I'd love to see you but I'm just walking out the door! What bad timing. Later.*

Thank God for quick voice texting.

Laura: *Since I'm near your street, I'll just drive by your house and wave to you as you leave. I miss you, girlfriend!*

She could only imagine the wild scene at Joan's house. Ben's car would be in her driveway, so would they hide his car or would she send him home?

Within a few minutes, Laura heard the garage door open.

# Chapter 3

Ben entered the house, threw his car keys on the table and stopped. "Laura?" He looked confused. "You're home?"

"I was out, but I just got home."

"Uh, shopping?"

"Not really. I was going to run by Joan's house, but since she texted that she was about to leave, I just came on home."

Ben relaxed, opened the refrigerator, and groused. "Why is there never anything to eat in this thing? I'm starved!"

"What happened to the boss furnishing dinner?"

"Uh, well, uh…his idea of dinner was, uh, was, uh, liver and onions. You know how I hate liver!"

Right. What boss would order liver for his overworked staff? No boss would, and from the chagrinned expression on Ben's red face, he knew it, too. Inwardly laughing at her husband's discomfort, she reached for her phone and started punching numbers.

Ben frowned. "Who are you calling?"

"Your boss! I want to know where he ordered the liver. He has such good taste so I would imagine he used a special restaurant. Not all chefs know how to cook liver."

Grabbing the phone out of her hand, he yelled, "You are *not* bothering my boss with such a ridiculous question!"

"Well aren't you the grouchy one! Something you want to talk about?"

"No, I don't want to talk!"

Laura shrugged. "That seems to be the story of my life. You won't talk, and lately my best friend doesn't seem to have time for me." She paused and then smiled as if she'd just had a good thought. "You know what I'm going to do?"

Ben was rooting around in the pantry. "No, but I'll bet you're going to tell me."

"I'm going to start dropping in on Joan."

A large can of white beans fell out of his hand and landed on his toes. "Goddamnmotherfucker!" he yelled, hopping around on one foot.

Laura turned her pleased face away from him.

After he recovered, he asked, "What do you mean, dropping in?"

"Without calling beforehand. Lately she always has an excuse why she can't see me and doggone it, I miss her!"

"B…but you can't do that!"

Smiling sweetly, she said, "Of course I can do that because she would be glad to see me. Joan and I grew up in each other's houses. We never called ahead, for heaven's sake! Good friends can do that."

The multitude of expressions that swept across his face told her that she'd hit a home run; she'd just made Joan's house toxic. Where were they going to go now? Motels take credit cards and cash. Credit cards leave a trail on the monthly statement, and with the budget Ben himself had authored, cash was closely monitored. Since he insisted that she stay home, they sure wouldn't be using this house.

Ben covered up his reaction to her statement by saying, "Since there's nothing to eat in the house, I'll just take a shower and go to bed hungry."

"Poor baby!" she cooed as she threw her arms around him. "I'm sorry your insensitive boss thought everyone liked liver." While hugging him, she buried her nose into his neck and sniffed. "Hmmm. I like the way you smell. Did you change your after-shave lotion?" She took another sniff. "Actually, it smells more like perfume."

His eyes widened. "You smell perfume?"

"Yes. It's really quite pleasant."

Ben ran up the stairs and slammed the bathroom door.

# Chapter 4

Laura's eyes flew open, surprised that she was waking up because she didn't remember going to sleep. At some point in the night, Ben had gotten tired of her tossing and turning and left to finish the night in the spare bedroom. Lately, he'd been disappearing in there several nights a week because, according to him, she kicked in her sleep. After what she'd discovered yesterday, she suspected that he wasn't sleeping in the spare bedroom because she disturbed him; he was there because he didn't want to sleep with her.

When the full realization of the state of her marriage hit, she panicked. Her world as she knew it was going to change dramatically. She hadn't worked since the birth of Teddy nine years ago, and technology had exploded in those years. Could she ever catch up and fit in?

Joan and John had gone through an expensive fertility clinic trying to become parents, but it hadn't worked. If Joan and Ben hooked up, would her used-to-be-best-friend fight to take Teddy and Beth away from her?

The more she thought, the angrier she became. Did they really think that good-old docile Laura would lay still while they ran over her?

When she threw her legs over the side of the bed, her foot came in contact with a warm furry creature.

"Good morning, Roscoe!" she greeted the dog. "I'll bet you have to go out." One thing she knew; Joan might get her husband, but she wasn't getting her children or her dog. She just needed to wake up the rusty and complacent brain that had gotten her two university degrees.

It was almost noon and Laura was still in her pajamas. Other than taking care of Roscoe, she'd done nothing but pace from room to room trying to make sense of her life. Her marriage was over. Even if

Ben's affair with Joan didn't turn into anything, she knew that he would just find someone else. The idea of marriage counseling wasn't something she would consider. While counseling might help the spouses stay together for the sake of the children, it couldn't generate love when it wasn't there to begin with. Ben just didn't love her anymore.

And Joan? What was her excuse? John traveled a lot, but Joan knew that when she married him. Granted, she probably was lonely, but with all the available men out there, why had she chosen the husband of her childhood friend?

The ping of her cell alerted her of an incoming text message. Looking around, she spotted her phone on the table beside her cup of cold coffee. The text was from Ben.

Ben: *Another late night. Since no one ate yesterday's liver, the boss promises to order something edible. Don't wait up for me. Love u*

She texted back:

Laura: *But I've cooked all morning! I felt so bad about your going to bed hungry last night. I know! I'll pack it all up and bring it to your office. Expect me in the next hour. Love u 2*

Another ping.

Ben: *No, no, do NOT show up at my office. We are all secluded in a conference room with a big Do Not Disturb sign on the door. Just save the food for tomorrow. Please don't get me in trouble with my boss! And I can't text anymore. love u*

She sat with the cell phone in her hands for a moment wondering what to do. Joan and Ben had to be somewhere, but where?

Joan dabbled in real estate whenever it pleased her. Not needing to work for money, she did it for the social end of the job. Getting to meet new people and driving them around in her big car was what Joan considered fun because it didn't matter to her if they bought anything. She was always pleasantly surprised when her casual sales pitch  sold a house. Listings required work so she didn't actively seek them, but since they seemed to fall into her lap, she hired an assistant to do the advertising, brochures, and open houses.

Laura had sincerely enjoyed watching Joan succeed as a realtor because good friends are never jealous over the other person's achievements. In fact, Joan entertained Laura with stories about her buyers and sellers. Some of them were local sports athletes, and one was even a famous Hollywood actor. While she was chasing Beth to remove Roscoe's bone from her mouth and arguing with Teddy who was insisting on playing hoops in the driveway during a thunderstorm, she'd listened and laughed as Joan would share her childless day.

Where were they? Laura sat down at the computer and pulled up the agency where Joan worked and clicked on their listings. Skimming through them, she was looking for either a vacant house or a furnished house to rent. Bingo! There it was. Joan had told her about the elderly couple who had died within two weeks of each other. Since none of the heirs wanted the house or anything in it, it was put on the market fully furnished.

Within the hour, a showered, shampooed, and dressed Laura pulled out of her driveway.

# Chapter 5

The house was easy to find. Sure enough, there were two cars parked in the driveway; one was Ben's family van, and the other was Joan's big flashy red Bentley. Since both of them would recognize her car, she pulled to the side of the street where a huge flowering decorative tree provided shade and some degree of concealment.

She didn't have to wait long. When the front door of the house opened, she grabbed her cell phone and slid low in the seat. With arms around each other, the couple walked toward their separate cars, kissed passionately, parted, and then drove off.

Laura took pictures.

Ben's text had said he had to work late, which to Laura had meant he would be spending the time with Joan. But it was only four o'clock and they had gone their separate ways. So, what was going on? After she turned around in a driveway, she followed Ben, and was surprised when he pulled into his office's parking lot.

He really was going to work late.

Back home, Laura downloaded the pictures to her computer, printed them, and placed them in a folder that she'd labeled "Roscoe's Records." Since Ben just tolerated the dog, there was a very slim chance that he would ever look inside the file. That done, a glance at the time told her she had long and lonely hours until bedtime. The thought of watching television or reading a book didn't appeal to her and after she played three games of FreeCell on her computer, she'd had enough.

If Ben divorced her, she'd have to go back to work. The thought excited her almost as much as it scared her. Would any employer even consider hiring her? What she needed was an updated résumé to hand to a prospective employer. She closed her eyes and thought. Somewhere, if her memory was right, there was a flash drive with saved documents from her old computer. There was a possibility that if she could find it, her old résumé would be on it.

No one had been in the attic for so long that the dust and spider webs made her wonder if the search was worth it. Spotting the box that more than likely would have the flash drive, she brushed the dust off the top and carried it down to the kitchen.

Once she opened the box, she was disappointed to see that the flash drive probably wouldn't be in it because the bundle of letters on top were from the year before she and Ben had married. His plan to tour Europe with some of his college buddies had been made before the two of them had become involved. Young love was strong, and although Ben reluctantly went through with the tour, his heart remained behind.

Remembering what Ben had written in his letters to her from Europe brought her a moment of sadness. What had happened to the love that had changed the course of their lives? Where had it gone? Laura dropped the bundle that suddenly felt hot in her hand. Since Ben didn't love her anymore, reading words that he'd written when he did would be too painful.

She was about to close the box when her eyes saw something little and red on the bottom of it. It was the flash drive.

# Chapter 6

Tears were making it hard for Laura to read the words that were on her computer screen. She was having trouble remembering the excited and confident girl who had written the résumé. What dreams she'd had! Closing her eyes, she tried to recapture the exhilaration and joy she'd felt while writing it. Her eyes flew open; dare she dream again?

No wonder Ben had fallen out of love with the woman she'd become. She had allowed babies, cooking, cleaning, car pools, play dates, and teacher conferences to smother the creative and vital creature that had attracted him at the beginning. Maybe the reason Joan had him now was because she hadn't changed from the carefree fun-loving person she'd always been. But then Joan never had to wrestle with babies, cooking, cleaning, car pools, play dates, and teacher conferences.

A pang of homesickness for Teddy and Beth came out of nowhere. How could she even think of laying the blame of what she'd become on motherhood? It was her fault that she just hadn't tried hard enough to remain her own person. Instead, she'd become complacent in the roles of wife and mother. The kids had one more week of camp, and then another week at the farm with Ben's parents. She had two weeks to change the course of her life.

It didn't take long to bring the résumé up to date. Her job as a graphic designer had ended two months before Teddy's birth, leaving the next nine years blank. Would an employer ever consider hiring her?

On another trip to the attic to return the box to its spidery home, she stopped to visit her stored artwork. Dusty blank and finished canvases, all with their faces turned away, leaned against the wall. At one point in her life, painting was all she lived for. "A day without painting is a day without sunshine" was her joyous motto, and the huge stack of her artwork here in the attic attested to the truth of the statement. It had been years since she'd held a brush in her hand. What had become of her passion? Everyone had raved about her talent, but had she really been that good? Would looking through her adult eyes at work that was done as a younger person tell her anything?

A half hour later, a very dusty and excited Laura left the attic carrying an easel, canvases, brushes and paint. Within minutes, she stood beside the easel that held a blank canvas, and closed her eyes. What to paint? Remembering how easily ideas used to flow, it puzzled her that her mind was as blank as the canvas. Maybe if she held a color-loaded brush in her hand inspiration would follow.

That's when she discovered that it wasn't just her inspiration that had dried up.

So had her paint supplies.

# Chapter 7

Ben bid Mike, his work partner, goodnight although it was way past midnight. The deadline for their project was noon so they'd made it, but only by a few hours. Mike was pissed about having to work so late and didn't hesitate to place the blame where it belonged...on Ben. Ben didn't even try to defend himself.

"What's going on with you?" Mike demanded.

Ben just shrugged.

"You know what?" Mike went on. "You remind me of my sixteen-year-old son. Just like you, he gets these telephone calls that turn him into a giggling girl."

Ben blushed. Giggle? He'd have to watch himself from now on. No sense in getting rumors started. He didn't need questions flying around, but Joan was all he could think about. Back at work after a rendezvous with her, he'd slip his unwashed fingers under his nose where her scent still lingered, and just like a sixteen-year-old, he'd walk around with an erection.

His house was dark when he unlocked the door and stepped inside. Laura usually left the hall light burning when he worked late, but not tonight. Finding his way through the family room to hit a light switch, his foot caught on something. The clatter and banging of things falling shattered the night's stillness.

"What the...?" Ben grumbled.

A light went on upstairs and Laura appeared at the top of the steps. "Ben?" she questioned.

In a sarcastic voice he answered, "You expecting someone else? Of course it's me! What's all this junk doing in the family room?"

"Sorry about that," she said as she turned to go back to bed.

"No, really. What is it?"

"Turn on the light, Ben."

Muttering to himself, he switched on a lamp to see what he'd tripped over. "Oh," he exclaimed. "You taking up painting again?"

"Maybe. I'm going back to bed."

14

"Sorry I woke you. I might just eat a bit of the dinner you wanted to bring to the office. I'm starved."

"Too late," she called over her shoulder. "It's gone."

"Gone?"

"Yes, gone. Roscoe and I ate it."

The closing of the bedroom door ended the conversation with an echoing thump.

# Chapter 8

Joan sighed, shrugged and reached for the tampon box. She was already behind schedule, and if anything else cropped up unexpectedly, she'd be late for her appointment with her psychiatrist, Dr. Zumwalt. He'd been really displeased with her the last time she'd been late, and he hadn't hesitated to tell her so. She really needed to talk to him today, but dare she tell him what she was doing with her best friend's husband? When she practiced putting it into words, she realized how sick it sounded. Even though Dr. Zumwalt knew that her craving a baby was making her crazy, he wouldn't approve. She just wouldn't tell him that even after another month of wild sex with Ben, she still wasn't pregnant. Her own husband was scheduled to be home during her fertile period this month and of course they would have sex. Since he hadn't gotten her pregnant in the many years they'd tried, she didn't hold any hope that this month would be different.

Ben wasn't going to like the news that sex wasn't going to happen while John was home. And he sure wasn't going to like it when she eventually had to tell him that all she ever wanted from him was a baby just like the two he'd given Laura. It wasn't fair that her best friend had two kids while she didn't have any. They'd talked many times about how great it would be if she had a Teddy and a Beth of her own. And how could she have a Teddy and a Beth unless Ben fathered them? Laura would understand, wouldn't she? She'd cried along with her when the very expensive efforts at the fertility clinic failed. Since there was no money left for another attempt, it was just logical to turn to the sperm bank that had fathered Laura's babies.

Ben was an enthusiastic participant, although he had no idea about his role in the affair. In fact, he was getting altogether too intense and possessive about the whole thing. After this was all over, she wanted Laura and Ben to still be the couple that she and John had always been close to. Ever since she had been Laura's bridesmaid and Laura had been hers, the two couples had combined their social lives. It was a comfortable arrangement of dinner dates, movies, an annual summer vacation at the lake, and impromptu picnics in the park. She never intended that the thing she had going with Ben would change anything. After all, since Laura didn't have a clue, why would anything be different? Lately, she'd noticed that Ben was acting as if what they were doing was a permanent thing. She'd give this arrangement a few more months, and then if he hadn't gotten her pregnant, she'd move on to someone else. Her thoughts went to one of her new buyers who had openly flirted with her behind his wife's back.

One last look at the clock sent her rushing to her car. If she disobeyed the speed signs, she should make it to Dr. Zumwalt's office on time.

# Chapter 9

It was late afternoon before Laura finished the painting. Her empty stomach was complaining, her arm was tired, but the colorful canvas on the easel was all she could think about. She hadn't lost it. In fact, the picture vibrated with the sense of strength and maturity that hadn't been evident in her youthful paintings.

Feeling pleased with herself, she removed her pajamas and stepped into the shower. As the hot spray washed away the day's accumulation of spattered paint, she imagined the complacency and lackluster of her old self washing away with the water as it rushed down the drain. Long forgotten dreams were filling her head and making her smile when the stray thought of dinner pushed its unwelcome way into the picture. Damn. Ben would be home in a few hours expecting her to have a hot dinner waiting for him. That was one of his earliest proclamations along with the one about, "No wife of mine is going to work outside the home."

What would happen if dinner wasn't waiting when Ben came home? Would the world end? But since the kids were gone and she'd had all day to herself, she couldn't come up with an excuse for not cooking. Promising herself that tomorrow she'd be stronger, she dried herself, dressed, and went down to the kitchen and turned on the oven. From the freezer, she took several pieces of chicken, dumped them into a baking dish along with a can of mushroom soup, and waited for the oven to heat. When it beeped, she slid the dish into the oven, made sure the paint was dry on the canvas, grabbed her purse and ran to her car. Dinner wouldn't be a gourmet meal, but it would have to do.

The studio, A Spot of Color, that had displayed and sold her paintings so many years ago, was just minutes away.

Ben stepped out of the bank's cool air-conditioned lobby into the muggy August heat with two new accounts in his pocket. He had to admit that he did feel a few qualms about going to another bank to hide money from Laura, but it was just something he had to do in his preparation for leaving her. Little by little he intended to siphon money from their joint checking and savings accounts to quickly build the balance in his new ones. Since she used their credit cards exclusively, the chance that Laura would ever notice the diminishing balances was slim.

His feelings for Joan were so strong, so new, and so deep that just being around his wife was becoming unbearable. The whole domestic package that included two kids, the wife, and a dog felt like an intolerable weight that was holding him away from his true love. Knowing that he could walk away from the package with no regrets was a surprise in a way, for at one time he had loved Laura.

He had just stepped out of the bank when the sight of his wife walking just a few yards ahead of him gave him a shock. What was she doing in town and what if she'd been by the bank's door when he'd walked out? Coming up with a reason why he was visiting a bank they'd never used would have put him in a difficult position.

Laura was carrying something. Curious, he followed her until she disappeared into a store. As he got closer, he saw all types of artwork displayed in the store's window. As far as he knew, she hadn't touched a brush since Teddy was born, so what was she carrying into A Spot of Color?

And then he remembered what he'd tripped over last night. Her painting supplies. Was she painting again?

# Chapter 10

Laura stood inside the art store breathing in the familiar smell that had been such an integral part of her past. A sense of comfort surrounded her, giving her the feeling that she'd just returned home. She was relieved to see that A Spot of Color was still owned by the same woman who was presently engaged in an intense conversation with an older gentleman she recognized as a local artist. As she watched, the conversation ended, the owner threw up her hands as if in defeat, and the man rushed past her on his way to the door. Laura gave the owner, Elizabeth Anderson, time to calm down before she ventured further into the store.

"Mrs. Anderson," Laura said as she approached the woman. "Do you remember me?"

It was obvious that the owner was still upset, but not too distressed to recognize her.

"Laura, is that you?" she cried. "Why, I haven't seen you in years!"

"Nine years, if you want to be exact," Laura replied.

"What have you been doing? Painting, I hope, but I sure haven't seen any of your work around here. Did you move away?"

Laura hung her head. "No, I didn't move away. I haven't been painting, Mrs. Anderson."

"Not painting? Is there something wrong? The Laura I remember wasn't happy unless she had a paintbrush in her hand. What happened?"

"Marriage," Laura answered. "Babies, cooking, cleaning, car pools, play dates, and teacher conferences. Life is what happened, Mrs. Anderson."

"But that's so wrong! A talent such as yours needs to be shared with the world."

Laura's face momentarily brightened. "You've just made my day! Thank you for your kind words."

Mrs. Anderson pointed to the canvas. "Are you going to let me see what's on it?"

Laura clutched the painting for a brief moment, suddenly reluctant to expose what her talent had turned into after years of neglect. What if Elizabeth took one look and then proclaimed that she no longer had it? Coming here was probably a bad idea.

"Something wrong, Laura?"

Laura hung her head and nodded. "Please remember that I haven't painted in nine years." Handing her the canvas, she added, "I just wanted someone to look at it and truthfully tell me if it's any good."

While Elizabeth Anderson studied the painting, Laura chewed on a thumbnail. The longer Elizabeth studied, the harder she chewed.

Finally, Elizabeth raised her eyes and smiled. "You can stop chewing now."

Laura dropped her hand. "Well?" Closing her eyes, she held her breath and waited for the blow to fall.

"I find it hard to believe that this is the first painting you've done in nine years. I'd say you've still got it, girl! Welcome back!"

"Really?"

"Yes, really."

Noticing a tear running down Laura's cheek, the owner asked, "What do you intend to do now? I certainly hope you will give yourself permission to have a life of your own. Raising children is wonderful! However, it looks as if you've allowed it to smother both you and your talent."

The picture of Ben kissing Joan that had been burned into her memory chose that moment to resurface. Straightening her shoulders, she announced. "What I intend to do now is to pick up where I left off. I have the next two weeks to figure out how I'm going to do that."

Elizabeth raised her eyebrows. "What's so special about the next two weeks?"

"My kids have one more week of summer camp and then another week with their grandparents. I'd like to have some kind of painting schedule set up before they return."

Elizabeth took one more look at the canvas before she made a decision. "Laura, just as before, I will be proud to display and sell your work in my store. However, right now I'm in need of an artist who is immediately available to take a commissioned job. A customer wants a painting of his summer cottage on Green Lake as soon as possible. His request is for a view of it from the water, so that would mean you'd have to go out on the lake to take pictures of the subject. Since he's downstate with his wife, I'm sure he wouldn't object to your using one of his canoes. Are you interested?"

A job? Elizabeth was offering her a commissioned job? Not trusting her voice, Laura just nodded.

"I've written the address on the back of his business card."

Laura took the card, looked at the front of it, and gasped. "Josh Lang, the writer?"

Elizabeth nodded. "Have you read any of his books?"

"Any? I've read all of them! He has a new one scheduled to come out in a couple of months and I've already placed an order for it. Oh, I'd love to meet him!"

"He and his wife live downstate in a Detroit suburb but he does his writing at the cottage. The lake residents are aware when he's here, but they've learned to leave him alone while he's writing. There are stories about those who thought they could drop in on him just because they were neighbors. The stories are fun to hear, but not fun for those who bothered him."

"Maybe if he likes my work, he'll autograph my book. Does he ever do that?"

"Oh, he's not a hermit. It's only during the writing period that he demands privacy. When his new book comes out, I'm sure he'll have a book signing event somewhere."

Laura almost giggled; life was getting more exciting by the minute. She'd never known a writer and here she was being commissioned to paint a picture for her favorite one. "Is there a reason for the rush job?"

"The lake cottage is their most special place on earth, according to Mr. Lang. However, Mrs. Lang is terminally ill and can't make the trip. Josh wants to give his wife a painting of the cottage before she passes."

Laura swallowed hard. "How sad. Of course I'm interested. I'll start tomorrow morning."

# Chapter 11

Josh Lang drove down the gravel road without the usual giddy anticipation of catching the first glimpse of the lake cottage. In former years, this last leg of the journey was filled with Marie's excited chatter, for this was her favorite place on earth.

When his five-hour-trip ended, he rested his head on the steering wheel and pondered his next move. Did he...or could he...bear to unlock the door and walk into the cottage that was filled with her? He shouldn't even be here while she was lying on a cold slab three hundred miles away.

Nothing seemed real. In his head, he knew Marie was gone, but his heart hadn't accepted reality. If only he'd been there to say the final goodbye. After years of dialysis, the end had come so suddenly that she'd died alone. He should have been with her, holding her hand as she passed, but he hadn't been. The day had started out with no hint that it would be Marie's last day on earth. Not being there to say goodbye was weighing heavily on his heart.

It bothered him that Marie had been adamant about being cremated. To him, burying an urn filled with her ashes seemed like such a cold thing to do. The funeral director was more than happy to solve the problem by selling Josh one of his deluxe caskets.

He had no words to explain why the urge to make this trip was so strong, but once the idea came to him, he knew he had to do it.

Marie had a collection of stones that she'd found on their many walks on the beach. To him, they all looked the same, but not to her. Each one had a story, and she remembered them all. Along with sand from their very own beach, she'd arranged them behind glass in a shadow box. This box and the urn holding her ashes would be tucked inside the casket that would be lowered into a hole in the ground...no! Even thinking about how it was going to feel three days from now when he actually watched this happening left him breathless.

But he was here, and he needed to grab the box and get back home as soon as possible. After taking a few deep breaths, he opened the car door and headed for the cottage.

His eyes, blinded by tears, never noticed the lone woman in a canoe just off shore.


Laura was proud of her success. Never had she launched a canoe all by herself, but here she was, paddling out from the cozy summer cottage, enjoying the experience.

It didn't take long to snap pictures from every angle, so it was with regret when she realized there was no reason to paddle around on the lake any longer. The sun was warm and the water was so placid that the urge to play a bit longer was strong until she remembered why Mr. Lang was in a rush to have the painting.

Grabbing the paddles, she was starting to head for the shore when she heard a popping sound. It took her a few seconds to realize the object now floating inside her craft was a plug, and water was bubbling up though a gaping hole in the bottom of the canoe. In her haste, she'd never even thought of grabbing a life jacket before pushing the canoe into the water. She could swim, but only for a short distance, and it sure wasn't a short distance to the shore. Did anyone besides Elizabeth even know she was out here? She and the canoe would sink, and there wouldn't be any trace of her left.

Panic set in.

"Help! Someone, help me!" she screamed, over and over. She didn't see it, but a curtain moved at one of the cottage's windows.

# Chapter 12

Josh was still trying to get the upsetting grave scene out of his head when he unlocked the door and stepped into the cottage…and stopped. The overwhelming sensation that he was not alone made the hair on the back of his neck stand up.

He was slowly backing out the door when the familiar, distinctive scent of Marie's perfume hit his nose. How could that be? For years, her four-hour dialysis treatment three times a week had kept her close to home and her trips to the cabin had been few and far between. His mind was playing tricks on him; if his nose smelled Marie's personally designed perfume, than that meant she was here. But she wasn't here, and she never again would be here. The finality of death hit him hard.

Coming here in the middle of making funeral arrangements probably wasn't a sane thing to do. A responsible man wouldn't have driven three hundred miles just to get something to tuck inside a casket, but a man who'd loved a woman as much as he'd loved Marie would. Even though he knew the box was important to her, he was still puzzled why the urge to make the trip had been so strong.

But since nothing seemed to be out of place, he shook off the feeling. He'd just grab the shadow box off the ledge above the fireplace and get back on the road.

It wasn't there; its place on the ledge was empty. The upsetting thought that he might have driven all those miles for nothing was disrupted by the increased intensity of Marie's perfume. The smell seemed to be coming from their bedroom.

When Josh entered the room, the first thing he saw was the shadow box on top of the nightstand. Beside it was a bottle of Marie's perfume on its side with its liquid contents puddled around it.

That's when he felt her.

"Marie?" he whispered.

She answered by sending him a wave of love so strong his legs buckled. Backing into the bed, he collapsed.

"You're here?"

The shadow box tipped over.

This wasn't happening. This couldn't be happening. He was too practical to believe that something like this was even possible.

And then, with one blink of an eye, her presence was gone along with the sweet odor of her perfume. He remained seated on the bed, unsure of what to believe. Had he imagined it because he needed closure? Or had Marie come to say goodbye?

He was about to pick up the box when he noticed that the completely sealed perfume bottle was standing upright; there was no sign of spilled liquid on the nightstand. His practical mind was struggling for an explanation when he noticed that the curtain on the picture window looking out at the lake was moving.

What he saw when curiosity got him to look out the window sent him running for the door.

Someone was drowning.

# Chapter 13

The shore looked no closer than it had when she'd started. How long could she keep this up? If only she could relax enough to tread water, but panic was starting to rear its ugly head, and when that happened, Laura knew that would be the end of her. *Just relax, relax, relax*, she murmured, trying to calm herself. Float. Yes, she knew how to float. All she had to do was not panic, lie on her back, paddle with her arms, and head toward the shore. Maybe if she sang. No, not sing, hum. Singing words would take too much effort and an open mouth would let in too much water. Thankfully, the water was warm.

What should she hum? It had to be a song that wasn't associated with either her cheating husband or her two-faced best friend. It was only because it popped into her head all by itself that she remembered a song about loving someone all the way that started *when somebody loves you*. Remembering the tune, she hummed while she floated on her back and paddled, hopefully, toward the shore.

She didn't hear the sound of a motor until it was quite close.

One glance out the cottage window was enough to send Josh running for his motorboat. Thank God he hadn't drained the gas out of it the last time he was here, and thank God he'd kept it in such good shape that it started on the first try. Whoever was out there flailing around in the water was in deep trouble. He only hoped the person would still be on the surface by the time he got there, because he wasn't the best diver in the world, and he'd hate for someone to drown just because he wasn't good at it.

Cutting the motor when he got near, he was surprised to hear, along with sputtered gasps for air, a woman's voice attempting to hum a melody. As he drifted closer, the shock of what he was hearing made him question his sanity. At a sorority party many years ago, that was the song the band was playing when he tapped a man's shoulder who was dancing with the prettiest girl in the room. The rest was history, but forever the song had remained *their* song.

First the shadow box, then the perfume, and now the song. Was he going insane?

The humming stopped when the woman became aware of the boat.

"Ahoy there!" he called. "I'm paddling to get closer. Don't panic, stay calm and I'll have you in my boat in no time."

Arms and legs flailed, and she disappeared.

Kicking off his shoes, he was preparing to dive when a head surfaced close enough for him to lean over the edge of the boat and extend his arm. "Here! Grab my hand!" The hand that seized his was a soft, very feminine hand.

"Hold on while I pull you in!"

It was hard to tell, but even with all the wet hair obscuring her face, he could see that she was an attractive woman. There wasn't much to her, so with very little effort he soon had her sitting across from him.

"Oh, th…thank yo…u!" Laura gasped. "I th…thought…," and then she burst into tears.

He looked around the boat for something to wrap her in, but of course there was nothing. Without a second thought, Josh removed his shirt. The shivering had turned into violent shaking and she was still sobbing. Trying not to rock the boat, he managed to cross the distance between them and sit down beside her.

"I'm s…so c…c…cold!"

It was the most natural thing in the world for Josh to pull her close to his warm body while he struggled to wrap her in his shirt.

That's when the aroma of Marie's perfume hit his nose. Startled, he dropped his arm and the unsupported woman grabbed the side of the boat to keep from sliding off the seat.

"Who are you?" he barked as he shied away from her.

"What?" She'd stopped crying.

"I'm asking you, who are you? And why are you wearing my wife's perfume?"

Laura looked in alarm at her savior. Yes, he had rescued her from drowning, but being in a boat with a crazy man might be as dangerous as drowning. She righted herself on the seat and glared at him. "What in the world are you talking about?"

"I'm asking you again! Why are you wearing my wife's perfume?"

"Sir, I have no idea what you're talking about. I don't ever wear perfume, and even if I did, do you think I'd still have any on?"

Other than acting peculiar, Laura had to admit that the muscular green-eyed blond man was quite good looking…and he *had* saved her life. "Sir?" She didn't like the way he was looking at her.

"Uh, I do apologize for what I'm about to do," he said.

Alarmed, she drew back. "And what are you about to do?"

"Smell you." With that said, he put his nose to her head, and sniffed. Nothing.

"It's gone," he said, flatly.

"What's gone?"

"Never mind." Maybe he wasn't crazy. "You still haven't told me who you are."

"Well, I don't know who you are, either."

He motioned to the cottage. "That's mine."

"Oh, then you are Josh Lang!"

"You know my name?"

Pulling the shirt a little closer, she nodded, "I'm Laura Baker, the artist that accepted the job of painting a picture of your cottage."

"Oh, so that's who you are." He sounded a little deflated. "And you needed to see it from out here?"

"My camera!" she cried, just remembering. "I lost my camera!"

"You were out here taking pictures of my cottage? I didn't ask for a photograph, I asked for a painted canvas."

"Sir, your request was for a view of your cottage from the water. How else was I supposed to know how it looked from the water? I took pictures to get the details right. Oh, by the way, it was one of your canoes that popped a plug. It's back there under the water along with my camera."

"No loss. That canoe was patched one too many times. And you can forget about the painting job. I've no need of it anymore."

If he didn't need the painting anymore, Laura reasoned, then his wife must have died. But it had to have just happened because it was yesterday that she'd been offered the painting job. So, what was he doing here, hundreds of miles away? Laura considered him a moment, noticing the bags under his eyes. Whatever the reason, thank God that he was because without him, she'd be dead by now. The sobering thought was interrupted when he continued.

"I'm in a hurry to get back downstate to arrange a funeral, so I hope you have transportation when I get you to shore."

So, his wife *had* died.

"Yes, my car is parked by your cottage. I'm surprised you didn't see it there."

"I've got other things on my mind right now, Miss Baker."

"It's Mrs. Baker," she corrected him.

"Okay, Mrs. Baker, but here we are back on shore, and that's as far as you and I go. Oh, and I'd like my shirt back. Have a good life."

Grabbing his shirt from around her shoulders, and his shoes from the bottom of the boat, Josh Lang walked away from a stunned Laura Baker.

# Chapter 14

Ben could feel his boss's eyes staring at him as he sat with his head down, pretending to read the meeting's agenda. The urge to pull his pinging cell out of his pocket and read the incoming text was hard to ignore, but his partner, Mike, had warned him. "I can't always cover your ass when you sneak out of here in the middle of the day. Mr. Turner is on to you, so watch it."

His boss was sitting across the table probably hoping that he'd be dumb enough to pull out his cell and answer the text. That's how close he was to losing his job.

His cell pinged again.

Ben squirmed in his chair, trying to make room in his pants for the activity that was going on down there. Joan had cut him off for the two weeks that John had been home, and it had about killed him. But now John was back on the road and he just knew that the texts that were coming in were from her, telling him where they could meet. The old couple's house had sold, but Joan was working on a new listing that would be perfect for them to use. She promised she'd text the address as soon as the listing was signed.

His body was responding by just imagining how it was going to be when they got together after being apart for two weeks. Closing his eyes, he savored the smell of her, the taste of her, the…

"Ben!"

His head jerked. "What?"

Mr. Turner was glaring at him. "God damn it! Why do you make me feel like a school-teacher? You can either participate in this meeting or you can share with the rest of us what must be a titillating daydream by the way you're squirming around. So, which will it be?"

Ben had the grace to blush. Fortunately, the boss's words had done what a cold shower was credited for doing.

"Sorry, Mr. Turner. It won't happen again."

"See that it doesn't!"

Ben wasn't answering her text. According to the reading on her thermometer, she was still ovulating. John had been no help. All he wanted to do in the time that he was home was sleep...just sleep.

She had other things to think about. Her psychiatrist was pulling things out of her that she wasn't ready to share with him. Up until recently, he had no idea how desperate she was to have a baby. It surprised her when she realized that she had been holding back information because she didn't want her psychiatrist to think she was crazy. But why else do you pay money to spill your guts to a complete stranger if you weren't?

If Ben wasn't going to answer her text, maybe she should check in with Laura. Lord only knew how often she'd ignored Laura's attempts to get together. Her texts usually arrived at a time when she and Ben were getting it on. Good thing Laura didn't know what they were doing.

Her thumbs got busy.

Joan: *Hey, girlfriend, been missing you. Coffee?*

Laura: *Busy. I'm painting again.*

Joan: *Good for you! I always wondered why you quit.*

Laura: *Ha. Spoken like someone who has never had kids!*

Joan: *Don't rub it in, girlfriend! I'm still trying.*

Laura: *Sorry about that. Had a near drowning experience. Would like to tell you about it, but not now. Gotta go. Bye.*


Ben seethed as the meeting continued. Mr. Turner had no right to embarrass him in front of his coworkers. Mike wasn't the only one at the table who was giving him a raised-eyebrow look.

*Fuck all of you!* he thought.

He tried, but he couldn't help but squirm in his chair while his boss's voice droned on and on. Did anything ever get resolved in these meetings?

When his mind wandered again, his thoughts were of Joan. She must be wondering why he hadn't responded to her texts. Maybe she was already at the new place, just waiting for him to follow the directions she'd sent in the texts that he couldn't read because he was being held prisoner in this stupid meeting.

His head jerked when he heard his name.

"What?"

"Is that all right with you?" Mr. Turner was asking him a question.

Taking a chance, Ben nodded his head in agreement.

"Of course."

"Good. I'm glad you've changed your mind. Now we can move ahead on the project. This meeting is adjourned."

Ben walked out of the room in a daze. What had he changed his mind about?

# Chapter 15

Laura woke up to a quiet house. Ben had gone to work and once again she was alone with just her dog for company. Teddy and Beth still had half a week of camp and a full week at the farm, giving her enough time to figure how she was going to make room in her busy schedule for painting.

She got as far as throwing back the covers before the recurring and terrifying fact hit her once again…she'd almost drowned yesterday. Collapsing back onto the bed, she gasped for air, much the way she'd done while she was trying to stay afloat. How long would she have lasted if Josh Lang hadn't shown up? She would have disappeared and no one would have known what had happened to her. Oh, eventually, her car would've been noticed, but since she hadn't told anyone that she'd been hired to paint a water view of a cottage, chances are that no one would figure out the puzzle until Mrs. Anderson noticed her missed deadline, or her body floated to shore. That was a shuddering thought.

Constantly on replay, the memory always started when the plug popped out of a patched hole in the canoe and warm water lapped around her legs. In a matter of seconds, what had been a pleasant day had turned into a panic-filled near-death nightmare. Just thinking about how hard it had been to stay afloat made her heart pound. She *had* remembered how to float, but how long would it have been before terror had taken over and made it impossible? Minutes?

It was hard to imagine a world without her. Teddy and Beth would be devastated for a bit until…until what? Until Joan took her place as their mother? *Over my dead body*, Laura fumed, even as she realized her poor choice of words.

Looking around the room, she tried to imagine how it would have been if she had drowned. Someone would've come in here after her funeral to sort through her things, making piles to discard, save, or take to Goodwill. Who would that have been? Ben wouldn't do it, but her pseudo good friend Joan would.

Laura pushed herself off the bathroom floor, wiped her mouth, and flushed the commode. It had taken the sickening picture of traitorous Joan going through her things to send her racing for the bathroom. Her old life was dead. Her marriage was over, and Joan, who had been her rock, her family, and the keeper of all her secrets, was now someone she didn't even recognize. Finding out that Joan really wasn't her best friend was making her question her own ability to see things as they actually were. How long had they been sneaking around? Ben, she could divorce, but Joan was a different problem. Joan was a part of almost every memory Laura had – not having that constant friend hurt more than the idea of losing her husband.

Maybe the near-death experience was a wake-up call to remind her that this life is not a dress rehearsal. From now on, things were going to be different. No longer was she a doormat to be walked upon. The touch of a cold nose on her arm chased away the morbid thoughts, reminding her that she was not alone. Wait a minute. If she had drowned, would Joan have gotten Roscoe, too?

That last thought was enough to propel her into the shower. Today, she had places to go and things to do. This new Laura would not wallow.


A Spot of Color was doing a brisk business when Laura arrived before noon. Elizabeth was busy at the cash register, smiling and chatting with the high-school art teacher who, by the look of it, had brought her entire class with her. It was hard to believe that fifteen years had passed since she had been one of them. Her head had been full of dreams that included four years of college and two more to earn an advanced degree, a painting career, and maybe marriage, but not before she'd become established as a recognized artist. She had been right on track until Teddy was on his way and Ben had reminded her of his proclamation. Why had she listened to him?

Teddy hadn't been an easy baby. There really hadn't been time for even a thought of putting a brush to canvas as she walked, sang to, and cried along with her colicky baby. Of course, Ben never offered to help. She was just coming up for air when she got pregnant with Beth.

Now, looking back on those years, she was surprised to realize that she didn't regret a minute of it. But that was then, and now it was her turn.

Elizabeth hadn't noticed Laura until the chattering students and their instructor had filed out the door.

"Laura!" she exclaimed, holding out her arms in greeting. "It's so good to see you again! Have you been waiting long?"

"To tell you the truth, I was enjoying watching and listening to the students. It brought back memories."

"I'll bet it did! But I'm dying to see the cottage painting! Did you bring it with you? Because it's a rush order, we need to get it to Mr. Lang as soon as possible."

Laura swallowed hard. "There's no painting."

Elizabeth's eyebrows shot up. "No painting?"

"Mr. Lang canceled the order; his wife is dead."

"She's dead? Well, that was sudden. He just placed the order two days ago." Elizabeth looked puzzled. "How did you find out? He couldn't have contacted you because he had no idea to whom I'd assigned the job."

"He was at the cottage."

"At the cottage? When he called me to order the picture, he was downstate with his very sick wife. So, you've met Josh Lang?"

Laura nodded. "I guess you could say that."

Elizabeth stepped back and took a good look at her. "Why am I getting the feeling that you're not telling me everything? What happened, Laura?"

The incident had left her with raw emotions so near the surface that just telling someone about it could open the floodgates.

"Could we go to your office?"

"Of course! I take it something bad happened?" she asked as she led the way.

Laura shut the office door. "I'm still shaking about it and I didn't want to alarm your other customers if I burst into tears."

"Oh, my!" Elizabeth exclaimed.

Laura surprised herself by managing to tell Elizabeth what had happened without breaking down. The only thing she left out was Josh's strange behavior. Demanding to know why she was wearing his wife's perfume hadn't made any sense then, and it sure wouldn't make any sense if she repeated it. The poor man was probably highly emotional and shouldn't be held accountable for his strange behavior.

Elizabeth looked puzzled. "I'm surprised that his wife died at the cottage because he told me that she was too ill to travel."

"Oh, she wasn't at the cottage. The last thing he said to me was that he has to go back downstate to make funeral arrangements."

At the end, Elizabeth hugged her. "That's quite a story. You said you wanted to meet him, and you sure did. The famous Josh Lang saved your life! How fortunate you are that he was at the cottage and not downstate with his wife!"

"Well, he was, and because he was, I'm here," Laura said as she rubbed goose bumps off her arm. "I'm having trouble with flashbacks that hit me when I'm least expecting them."

Elizabeth paused for a moment, thought about her options, and then made a decision. "Laura, I think the best thing you can do right now is to keep so busy the flashbacks won't have a chance to upset you."

"I agree, but the kids are still gone, and Ben works long hours. It's hard to fill that much time."

"I may have a solution to your problem…that is, if you are really serious about painting again."

"Oh, I intend to paint, Elizabeth! I'm just not sure what I want to paint. I can do portraits, still life, and scenery, but since I soon might have to support myself, I need to pick a venue that sells."

"To support yourself?" Elizabeth looked surprised.

Laura lowered her eyes. "Unfortunately, it's looking that way." Raising her eyes, she added. "I'd appreciate it if you'd keep it a secret."

"Of course."

"But you said you had a solution?"

Elizabeth nodded. "Remember the first day you dropped in? I was talking to Paul Wise, a local artist."

"I was watching. It looked like you two were disagreeing about something."

"It really wasn't a disagreement…or maybe it was. He wants to leave and I was trying to talk him out of it. Paul has been my resident artist for years. We live in a vacation area, a place where people come for a few weeks or months out of the year and then go home with beautiful memories. There's always a demand for pictures to be painted of their boats, their summer home, and sometimes they want a winter painting of their place. That's what Paul did. Over the years, he made enough money to send his two girls to college. But now he and his wife want to retire somewhere away from our cold and snowy winters."

Laura's eyes were shining. "And you need a replacement for Paul?"

"Does that sound like something you'd want to do?" Elizabeth asked.

"Yes, yes, yes!" Laura cried. "It's exactly what I want to do!"

"Good! Your first assignment was the Lang cottage, but that didn't have such a good ending, did it?"

"Well, Josh's wife dying wasn't good, but I didn't drown, and that's good! When do I start?"

"I have two commissioned, and a possible third. I'll give you the addresses and the requests and you can start whenever you want. There's no rush on either order!"

# Chapter 16

Joan pulled into the driveway of a beautifully maintained Cape Cod that had her name on a For Sale sign in the front yard. The owners had interviewed several realtors before awarding her the listing based on her assertion that she had a buyer for the property.

And she did. The house and the wooded setting fit all the criteria cited by her buyers when she started working with them four weeks ago.

The fact that the husband had shown his immediate attraction to her tall slim body didn't surprise her. Because most men reacted this way when they first saw her, she'd become quite adept at putting them in their place. If she hadn't yearned for a baby so desperately, she could have easily shot down his advances, but she'd encouraged them. She'd hoped that today he would behave himself and forget about the afternoons of wild sex they'd shared, but she'd hoped in vain. It was obvious he'd taken the afternoons very seriously by the way he was sniffing around her as if she were a bitch in heat. Damn! She never should have gotten involved with a buyer.

Trying to ignore him, she exclaimed, "Mr. and Mrs. Carter, I think you're going to love this one!"

Mrs. Carter didn't look at the house or move from her position in the car; instead, she stared at her husband. It was evident by the way Henry was acting that there was something going on between him and the realtor. She'd hoped that the marriage counseling she'd dragged him to for the past six months had put an end to his roving eye, but apparently, it hadn't. If he only knew how ridiculous he looked!

As soon as the car stopped, Henry rushed around to open Joan's door before she had a chance to open it herself. "Here, let me help you," he said, extending his hand.

Joan looked into his lust-filled eyes and cringed. First Ben and now Henry. What happened to the premise that all men liked casual sex with no strings attached?

Henry didn't allow her to pull her hand out of his grasp. His eyes sought hers, hoping to see signs that she was just as eager as he was for another romp in bed. Their secret trysts had blown him away. He'd forgotten how great sex could be with the right partner, and since no amount of counseling had turned his wife into one of those, all he could think about was hooking up with Joan again. That's what he thought she was calling about today, but to his disappointment, it wasn't. She wanted to show them a house that had just come on the market.

Joan pulled her hand away, and without moving her lips, she hissed, "Stifle it, Henry. Now go help your wife."

Henry tried to hide his disappointment. Stifle it? The woman who'd left scratch marks on his back and bite marks on his neck was telling him to stifle it?

Even before he turned to look at his wife, he could feel her eyes burning him. Hell, she was on to him. He thought he'd successfully covered the marks Joan had left but maybe he hadn't. Opening her door, he tentatively offered her his hand.

"Don't touch me," she snapped.

The tour through the house was made in total silence. Joan knew she was not going to be selling a house to the Carters even though the house and property had everything they said they wanted. Mrs. Carter wasn't even pretending to look while they toured the rooms.

Damn! She'd screwed up. Getting sexually involved with Henry had been a bad idea, and she knew it even while it was happening. If she hadn't been so desperate to have a baby, it never would have occurred. But it had, and now she would have nothing to show for all her work. For four weeks, she'd chauffeured them from house to house with a few meals thrown in if the showings ran through the eating hour. Now her buyers would just go to another realtor and buy the house.

And the silence continued during the ride back to the office where the Carters had left their car. It was finally broken when Gertrude rolled down the car's window as they prepared to drive away. Henry was looking straight ahead when she called to Joan, "We no longer need your services."

# Chapter 17

The morning had slipped away so pleasantly that Laura was surprised when her stomach growled. The past four hours had been filled with such contentment that she hadn't noticed the passing of time.

Stepping back from the easel, she viewed her work. The lake home seemed to take on a life of its own. She could almost smell the roses that grew on vines that crawled along the white picket fence. Pleased with what she had created, she felt good as she headed for the kitchen. After lunch, she could finish it with just a few more hours of work.

While she was waiting for the soup to heat, it dawned on her that the flashback of her near-drowning experience wasn't catching her off-guard as frequently as it had been. What she *had* been thinking about was Josh, the man who'd saved her. There wasn't a reason in the world why she would ever see him again, but if she did, there were a few questions she'd love to have him answer…after he'd signed her book. What was he doing hundreds of miles away from his dead wife, and what was that bit about her smelling like his wife's perfume? She told herself that his being extremely handsome had nothing to do with her thoughts.

The pinging of the microwave brought her back. Ben wasn't sending text messages about working late anymore, but something must be going on. His disposition was ugly, his patience was nonexistent, and he didn't even bother to make up an excuse when at bedtime he chose the spare room.

Ben had no idea that she was aware of his affair with Joan, but she knew that if she confronted him about it, the marriage would be over. Since she needed more time to paint and build up a reserve of money before she and her children ventured out on their own she planned on playing along like the naïve wife Ben thought she was.

Even knowing that Ben was cheating, she could live with him for a bit longer, but what was she going to do about Joan? Until just recently, the two of them had been inseparable. For years, frequent telephone calls, luncheons, shopping trips, dropping in to visit unexpectedly, and spur-of-the-moment pot-luck dinners were woven into the fabric of their lives. Lately this hadn't been true. Joan hadn't even responded when she told her she'd nearly drowned. In the past, Joan would have rushed to her, hugged her, and cried with her. Maybe she was feeling guilty after all. Eventually they were going to be in the same room together. What then?

She'd finish up the one painting in time to have Ben's dinner on the table when he got home from work. Well, she *was* going to work outside the home, and the days of her having hot food on the table when he got home from work were numbered.


Ben would never admit that he was stalking Joan, but when she informed him that she couldn't see him because she had an out-of-state buyer, that's exactly what he did. He followed them and while parked down the street, he wondered why it took so long for the buyer to inspect a vacant house. And then the next two days Joan and the buyer spent a lot of time in other vacant houses. The fourth day, Ben saw the guy enter her office with a woman on his arm. Within minutes, Joan and her customers came out of the office and drove away in Joan's car. Since his lunch hour wasn't over, he followed them to see which vacant house the husband had picked to show his wife.

When Joan pulled her Bentley into the driveway of a very large house in an affluent neighborhood, realization struck. All those afternoons in those vacant houses she'd been screwing her buyer's brains out. The memory of how it felt to be on the receiving end of Joan's ministrations left him breathless. How could she do this to him? The pain of how Joan had enticed him to betray his wife hit with such force he closed his eyes and squeezed the steering wheel. The bitch! And to think he was about to ask Laura for a divorce! He'd been willing to walk away from his wife, his home and his two kids for this slut?

The more he thought about it, the angrier he became. Because of Joan, the threat of being fired from his job was real. Mike was getting tired covering for him at work and his boss was none too happy with him after he messed up the last project. It was all her fault. Up until Joan, his dalliances outside the marriage had been just one-night stands. As long as Laura didn't know about them, it was no big deal. Don't most men cheat?

It had been different with Joan. He'd felt it, but evidently she hadn't. She obviously had no qualms about screwing her best friend's husband.

She needed to be punished.

# Chapter 18

Just as Josh had pictured it, he watched Marie's casket being lowered into the ground. His knees buckled, arms encircled him, and voices murmured words of sympathy, but since he was in his own private hell, he neither felt nor heard any of it. This couldn't be happening. It was all a bad dream, a nightmare that would soon be over. He just had to wake up.

He heard nothing of the graveside service, but when friends first threw flowers on top of the casket and then followed with a handful of dirt, he'd lost it and had to be physically restrained. Gentle hands tried to lead him back to the car, but he refused to go. There was no way he was leaving Marie. How could he? What happened next was always a blank spot in his memory, and try as he might, he never was able to remember how he'd made the journey from the cemetery to his house. He had barely managed to function at the gathering of friends for the light lunch prepared and served by his neighbors.

But now everyone was gone, and he was left with a house that although it was deadly devoid of noise, it screamed loudly about the absence of Marie. Standing in the middle of their bedroom, he closed his eyes and tried to feel her presence. He felt nothing.

"Marie, don't leave me!" he whispered.

The image of the overturned shadow box and the remembrance of the essence of her perfume filled his mind. She was at the cottage! Grabbing his keys, he headed for the garage. If Marie was at the lake, that's where he should be.

Daylight was slipping away but Josh made no motion to go inside. Maybe if he sat out here long enough looking at the lake, Marie would join him. For the past three days he'd been sniffing, hoping to smell her perfume. But no matter how much he wanted to see some manifestation of her, it hadn't happened.

Dusk at the cottage was always her favorite time of the day. She would have a bottle of water and he would drink a beer while they waited for the fiery ball to sink into the lake. Marie would tell him about her trip into town for groceries and he'd read to her the chapters he'd written. Sometimes she'd comment about what his characters were doing and ideas for expanding the plot. Since she was the only person who ever saw his manuscripts before he sent them off to the publisher, he listened. So astute was she to his market, he was fully aware that her suggestions kept him from straying outside the comfort zone of his readers. Who was going to listen to him now? Without Marie, he felt vulnerable.

He'd struggled to write, but his fingers were reluctant to type. Sometimes he managed a page or two, but when he read what he'd written, disgust would make him hit the delete key. The fact that a publishing deadline was approaching didn't help; inspiration can't be forced. Ideas that usually came so easily here at the lake were eluding him. Characters, who in the past had taken over the story and interacted with each other, were silent.

Is that what Marie was? His muse? That thought was so scary, he choked on his beer. Writing was his bread and butter, how he made his living, and the only skill he had to support himself. Had his writing career ended with Marie's death?

It was the pitch-black moonless night that finally sent Josh back inside. The sound of glass hitting glass when he tossed his empty bottle in the direction of the growing pile of them made him flinch. Without Marie around, in just a few days he'd managed to trash the cottage. The light from a floor lamp revealed a sink full of dishes, pans on the stove that were crusted with dried food, and clutter covered the floor.

Josh's world was falling apart.

# Chapter 19

All Ben's thoughts of punishing Joan for cheating on him fled with one phone call from her. Her description of what she was going to do to him the next time they got together had him so hot he had to disappear into the men's room to take care of the problem.

Mike had made it quite plain that he was through making up stories about why he was not at his desk. But even knowing that he was putting his job in jeopardy, there was nothing in this world that was going to keep him from meeting Joan at her new listing. She was what gave color to his life, oxygen to his lungs, and a purpose to his existence.

Without a second thought, he grabbed his keys and headed for the parking lot. In his pocket he had the address of Joan's new listing where she was waiting for him.

The afternoon traffic was light and driving was so easy that he let his mind wander. So what if Joan had cheated on him? He really hadn't expressed his love for her in words. As soon as she understood the depth of his feelings for her, he had no doubt that she'd forget all about the buyer and John, her husband. He grinned at the thought of how happy he was going to make her when she understood that he was willing to give up everything just to be with her.

That led to the sobering thought about Laura. How much fight would she put up to save their marriage? Sure, he'd miss Teddy and Beth, but he'd have visiting rights, wouldn't he? And then there was the matter of child support that he'd have to pay every month. Would he have to support Laura, too?

His mind switched to Laura's near-drowning event. If only she hadn't been rescued! What an easy way out of his marriage that would have been. Oh, he'd given her a big hug and said how glad he was that she'd been saved, but what if that writer fellow hadn't been there? Becoming a bereaved husband would have been a quicker way out of his marriage and a lot less messy than a divorce. But it hadn't happened.

He looked at the dashboard clock and squirmed. In just fifteen minutes he'd be with Joan. She was probably there already naked, waiting for him. Since she was into foreplay, within minutes of his getting there she'd have his clothes off and be doing delicious things to his body. Distracted by sensuous thoughts, his attention wandered.

Sitting high in the cab, the driver of an eighteen-wheeler approached the intersection with caution. His light was about to turn green, which meant the crossing lane's light would be turning red. Years of trucking had made him a defensive driver, always watching for a sign that a problem was possible. With the exception of one car, he could see that all the cross traffic was coming to a stop as their light was changing to red. That one car was going to be a problem. It's hard to stop an eighteen-wheeler, but he tried.

Ben was in the middle of a delicious sexual fantasy when the truck smashed into his car.

# Chapter 20

The scene at the prison was wild. Fingers were pointing, accusations flying… the most frequent one being, "I told you so!"

Their model prisoner had not only escaped, he'd left behind a dead guard, Larry, one of his own Bible study followers.

Behind closed doors, the warden was fuming. "So, what do you think of your poster boy now? You do-gooders and your rehabilitation nonsense! Did you really believe that a serial killer could change?"

Reverend David, one of the prison's ministers, hung his head. "I honestly never saw this coming. George has been a changed man for years! His is the largest Bible study group in here."

The warden huffed. "Who gave him permission to get out of his cell today?"

A white-collared cleric cleared his throat. "If you haven't been noticing, George has had free run of this prison for the past couple of years. The guards know him by name, and all they do when they see him out of his cell is nod to him. So, who gave him permission? Larry probably knows, but unfortunately, Larry isn't talking."

The warden looked worried. "The press is going be asking question about my lax policies. I could lose my job over this!"

Rev. David bowed his head. "I think the important thing right now is to pray for his capture before he kills another woman."

The warden nodded. "You're right. Maybe someone will notice that the driver of a police van is wearing an orange suit."



Life was good! Laura couldn't keep the smile off her face as she set the table with her good china. Tonight was going to be a celebration of her emancipation from Ben's edict. She wasn't going to ask permission to go back to work; she was going to *tell* him that she'd already accepted a job. Just let him try to say she couldn't do it! If things got a little testy, maybe she'd have to hint that she knew about his affairs. She wouldn't even have to mention what he was doing with her friend because she was sure that Joan wasn't his first digression.

The smell of roasting chicken followed her to the shower and then to her dressing table where she applied make-up and arranged her hair the way Ben liked it. When she finished, the mirror reflected not a housewife, but a professional and competent woman who was ready to defend her declaration of freedom.

She was heading for the kitchen when the doorbell rang. A glance at the clock showed her that it was much too early for Ben to be home. Anyhow, he had a key, so he wouldn't be ringing the doorbell. Joan? Maybe Joan was doing one of their drop-in visits that they used to do all the time. Her breath caught in her throat. How could she look Joan in the eye, knowing what she and Ben were doing? Maybe she just shouldn't answer the door.

The doorbell rang again.

Standing sideways so whoever was ringing her bell wouldn't see her, she peeked through the curtain. What she saw instantly caused a wave of terror to knock the wind out of her; a uniformed policeman was standing on her porch. Something bad had happened to Teddy or Beth.

Opening the door was hard. Whatever message the man was bringing, she had the feeling that her life was going to be changed forever.

"Good afternoon," he greeted her while holding up a badge. "I'm Sergeant Davis. May I come in?"

Unable to talk, she just nodded.

Once inside, he asked, "Are you the wife of Benjamin Baker?"

So, it wasn't about her kids! A quick feeling of relief came and went.

"Yes, I am. Why do you ask?"

"I'm sorry to tell you that there's been an accident…"

"Ben?" Laura's eyes were wild. "Something happened to Ben?"

"Yes, he was involved in an accident on route M-72 just south of town."

"Is he okay? Is he in the hospital?"

Sergeant Davis swallowed hard. He hated this part of his job. "Mrs. Baker, your husband didn't survive the crash."

"Wait a minute!" she cried. "You're saying that Ben is dead? My husband is dead?"

"Unfortunately, yes. Your husband was killed instantly when a truck hit his car."

Alarmed by the woman's swaying body, he reached out his hands to steady her. "Maybe you'd better sit down, Mrs. Baker. Is there someone you can call?"

Thinking of her best friend who had been a big part of her life since grade school, she nodded.

And then, she remembered.

"Uh, no. I have no one to call."

"Mrs. Baker, eventually you will have to accompany me to the morgue to identify his body."

Laura backed up to a chair and collapsed.

# Chapter 21

It didn't seem real. Ben was dead. Searching her memory, she tried to remember the last time she'd seen him. Since he'd been sleeping in the spare bedroom, some mornings he'd leave the house while she was still in bed. She didn't even want to think of what he and Joan were doing on nights when he claimed he was working late. It was the unfairness of it all that kept switching her emotions from one of extreme sorrow to one of instant rage. How dare he leave her to cope with life on her own!

The first call had been the devastating one to Ben's parents. How do you cushion the message that their only son is dead when you're sobbing so hard they can't understand you?

Within hours, his parents arrived, bringing Teddy and Beth home with them. Soon her once empty house was filled to capacity with Ben's relatives.

She moved through the days in a state of detachment, feeling at times that this had to be a bad dream. But life has a way of going on, and she had guests to feed. It was when she was in the middle of preparing lunch for six relatives and two children that the front door opened and slammed shut. The sound of heels hitting the hardwood floor alerted her that someone was heading for the kitchen. It was probably another one of Ben's relatives dropping in looking for food.

She turned around from the stove just as Joan rushed into the room.

It wasn't that it was surprising that she'd walked into the house without ringing the doorbell, because it wasn't. Best friends can do that. But the Joan who was trying to hug her now was not her friend anymore.

Throwing her arms around Laura, Joan gushed, "Oh, you poor thing! I came as soon as I heard the awful news, but why didn't you call me? I had to hear about Ben from a neighbor!"

All the plotting and planning of the subtle ways she was going to make Joan's life miserable fled out of her head. There was fury in her eyes when she tore Joan's arms from around her neck.

A surprised Joan cried, "Why, Laura! What's wrong? Oh, Honey! You must be so upset!"

Laura reared back and looked Joan in the eye. "You are not welcome around here anymore. Get out!"

Joan had the audacity to look puzzled. "Get out?"

"You heard me. Get out. I don't want you here."

Joan stepped back, her face crumbling. "I can't believe you said that to me! What's wrong? I'm your best friend, Laura. I loved Ben, too."

Laura's eyes narrowed. "You were also screwing him, Joan."

"Wh.. wh..what?"

"Oh, don't look so surprised!"

Joan's face turned white. "You knew?"

"Of course I knew! I'm not as naïve as you and Ben seem to think I am."

"So, then it was okay with you?" Joan blew out a big relieved breath. "I knew you'd understand!"

"Understand?" Laura stepped back, and there was a look of complete puzzlement on her face. "What the hell are you talking about? What do I understand?"

"Laura, think back. How many times have we talked about my having a Teddy or a Beth of my own? Think about it! To get a Teddy or a Beth I'd need Ben to father them, wouldn't I?"

Laura's mouth dropped open. "Did Ben agree to do this?"

"Ben? No, he didn't have a clue."

Laura took a closer look at Joan. True, the two of them had talked many times about Joan being childless and they'd clung together through the costly but failed fertility tries, but until this moment Laura had no idea that Joan's obsession to have a baby ran this deep.

"Let me get this straight. You thought that having sex with Ben would be okay with me because I wanted you to have kids just like mine?"

"Well, don't you?"

"Joan, do you have any idea how sick that sounds?"

"No, no! Don't say that!" Joan's face contorted. "I'm not sick! But you…you…are my best friend! I can't believe you don't understand!"

Laura pointed her finger toward the door. "Get out of here, Joan! I don't have time for this crazy conversation right now. You are not welcome around here anymore."

"Please, Laura! Don't do this!"

"Joan, if you think what you did with my husband was a rational thing to do, then you're a very troubled woman who needs professional help. Now excuse me, I have to make arrangements for a funeral."


Get out? Joan stood outside Laura's front door and fumed. During their long friendship, there had been many little spats, but nothing like this. Dr. Zumwalt had been right all along; using her friend's husband for what amounted to nothing more than stud service went way beyond the bounds of rational reason. She should have listened, but she hadn't. So now, what? Ben was dead, and Henry's wife was onto him. The need to have a baby in her arms hit her with such force her legs buckled. Grabbing hold of the porch rail, she flopped down on the top step and with her empty arms, hugged herself.

A male voice broke into her miserable state. "Are you okay, lady?"

Startled, Joan raised her eyes. Standing in front of her was a tall, uniformed and outrageously handsome specimen of the male gender. In his hand was an arrangement of flowers, someone's thoughtful gift for the widow. Her teary eyes turned into flirty ones in a matter of seconds, and with a seductive smile on her face, she rose out of her sitting position slowly enough for the man to observe and appreciate her body.

When Laura peeked through the curtain to see who was ringing her doorbell, she saw more than a uniformed deliveryman holding a large bouquet of flowers. She'd thought Joan had gone when she kicked her out of the house, but she hadn't because she could see her used-to-be-best friend crawling into the passenger side of the florist's truck.

The bell rang insistently, the way it would ring if a finger were holding down the button. Laura didn't blame him. The deliveryman probably wanted to get back to his truck and check out the crazy lady who had just crawled into it.

Laura opened the door.

Without a word, he thrust the flowers at her, turned, and ran back to his truck. Laura shook her head. What was Joan up to now?

Holding the flowers in her arms, she stood by the window and watched Joan wave to her as the truck pulled away from the curb.

# Chapter 22

George Knox's eyes left the road long enough to take in the sight of the absolutely stunning blond who had crawled into his truck. She was a little old for his taste, but who was he to turn down an unexpected gift? The familiar desire that had been waiting years for release stirred in his belly. Who she was and why had she hitched a ride with him wasn't important.

Trying to contain his excitement, George spoke calmly. "Well, isn't this my lucky day!"

"Do you mind?" the pretty lady asked, coyly.

"Mind? I'm honored!"

Sliding across the bench seat to be closer, the woman reached out a hand and put it on his knee.

George's reaction caused the truck to leave the road, narrowly missing a mailbox.

"Sorry about that," he muttered.

Joan wriggled. She'd found herself a live one. And so handsome! The babies they would make together would be so much better than Teddy and Beth. Laura was going to be *so* jealous.

Her hand moved a bit closer to his crotch.

He slammed on the brakes. "Lady, are you asking for trouble?"

"I certainly hope so," she breathed into his ear. "Do you have time for a quickie?"

George was having trouble breathing. "You have a place in mind?"

"I have a great place in mind. Turn left at the next light."

"And just where are we going, pretty lady?"

"My house," Joan replied.

Following her directions, George's heart beat wildly while he drove through what had to be one of the more expensive sections of the town. The houses were big and set back off the road in the middle of green well-tended yards. The woman was pointing to the largest one on the block.

"Pull in here. I'll run inside and operate the garage door opener. Might as well hide your truck. Neighbors can be so nosy!"

What kind of luck was this? He needed a place to hide until he could come up with a plan, and what better place than this? The garage door was slowly opening and the time for wondering was past. Putting the truck into gear, he drove it into the garage and parked beside a red Bentley.

The woman was waiting for him when he stepped out of the truck. "By the way," she said as the garage door closed, "my name is Joan."

Should he tell her his real name? Oh, what the hell. What was happening was so surreal, he was probably still in prison having one of his great fantasies. There was little chance that she'd remember newspaper headlines along with pictures of him on Most Wanted posters. But so what if she did? She wasn't going anywhere.

And then he remembered why he couldn't use his own name.

"Dave. My name is Dave," he said, pointing to the name stitched into the pocket of the uniform.

"Well, Dave, are you hungry?"

He opened his mouth to answer when he remembered the orange suit that was under the uniform. If she saw it, the party would get rough before it had to. "I'd love something to eat! Could I possibly use your bathroom to clean up?"

"Yes. While you're gone, I'll whip us up an omelet. Use the bathroom off the master bedroom. It's the last room at the end of the hall."

This lady is crazy, he thought. Even crazier than I am.

When the orange suit was stuffed into an opaque garment bag that he'd found in the back of the closet, George returned to the kitchen.

"Have a seat."

George eyed her offering. "Looks good!"

While filling his plate with a huge pile of scrambled eggs, she winked at him. "Eat up! You're going to need a lot of energy for what I have planned for us."

George smirked. The lady had no idea.

# Chapter 23

Ben was dead. He was dead when she went to bed at night, and he was still dead when she woke up in the morning. It had to be a bad dream, but no matter how hard she tried, she couldn't shake herself awake. Feeling as if she were operating in very thick mud, she managed to drag herself through the motion of feeding and caring for her houseguests, assuring herself that they would be gone in a few days.

Beth and Teddy were another story. Not understanding the finality of death, they were sure he'd eventually come back because he loved them too much to stay away.

Ben's funeral was well attended. More of his relatives showed up, some of whom Laura had never met. He must have been well liked at work because their number almost filled the church. As for Laura, several of her artist friends and a few high school acquaintances that still lived in the area showed up. She had no relatives.

All she knew about her parents' deaths she'd gotten from reading the police and emergency crew's report of the accident. With the apparent help of a Good Samaritan, she'd been born at the scene of the crash. The emergency crew who responded to the call had found two dead adults and one crying baby wrapped in a blanket. The person who had stopped to help with the delivery never came forward, and with no identification on the dead couple driving a stolen car, the search for the truth ended. When no family member could be found, an eager young couple became her adoptive parents. Laura had tried over the years to uncover more information, but back then the ability to gather and analyze DNA hadn't existed.

Bill and Rose Roberts had been wonderful parents. However, they had sent flowers along with a note expressing their sympathy and a statement saying that because of Bill's medical problems, they would not be attending the funeral.

If Joan showed up, Laura hadn't seen her.

Joan pushed his heavy leg off her body, untangled the sheet, and crawled out of bed. Just looking down at the beautiful man in her bed made her hot. Seeing his impressive package stirred up desire that should have been sated considering what they'd done before they both passed out from exhaustion. The urge to wake him was strong, but she wouldn't. He needed his rest because she wasn't finished with him.

Sex with the guy had been a big surprise; it was like no other sex she'd ever had. Not once had she had to fake an orgasm, and she'd had more of them in one afternoon than she'd had with any of her other lovers put together. With him, sex was a whole new ball game and she was planning on playing a lot more innings.

On her way to the shower, she had an unsettling thought. He was a workingman with a boss who probably wanted his van full of flowers back. What if he insisted on leaving when he woke up?

No, no! That was not going to happen until she was ready for it to happen. She had the house all to herself until the end of the week when John came home. Since she no longer had a best friend, no one was going to drop in unexpectedly.


George was between waking and sleeping when he felt Joan slip out of bed. Keeping his eyes closed, he marveled at the turn of events that had brought him here.

The morning had started out like every other morning in the ten years he'd spent behind bars. Since Michigan didn't have the death penalty, he had no reason to think that the rest of his mornings on this earth would be any different. For good reason, his sentence had been life without parole.

Every night he lay on his bunk, a pillow over his head to shut out the night sounds of disgruntled inmates, and tried to figure out a weakness in his daily routine. There had to be one, because he was not going to die in prison. Even if he failed in his attempt to escape, what did he have to lose? Since he was in prison for life and there was no death penalty, what more could they do to him?

He'd never paid much attention to the prison ministry until he noticed that several inmates who actively participated seemed to have more privileges than other prisoners. The next time he had a chance to speak to one of them, he asked about it.

"Why, all I had to do was to let Jesus Christ into my heart and then attend Bible study."

This didn't make sense to George. "There has to be more to it than that."

A guard pushed between them. "Move along there!"

George shrugged, resigned to the fact that if he wanted to know what was going on, he had to be more observant.

Intrigued by the presence of one man who wasn't a member of the clergy, but who showed up as often as they did, George flagged down Larry, one of the guards.

George pointed to the man. "That guy there. I see him here all the time. What's he up to?"

"He's a social worker."

George smirked, "One of the do-gooders?"

Larry nodded. "I talked to him the other day. Seems there's some kind of long-term study going on in here. The theory is that teaching inmates a trade or a skill will help them make it on the outside once they've been released."

George threw his head back and laughed. "So now they think they're going to rehabilitate us by teaching us how to make ashtrays in a pottery class?"

"It's more than that. There are prisoners in here who once were teachers, artists, mechanics, writers…you get the idea? The plan is to use their skills instead of hiring outsiders."

"They're letting prisoners out of their cells to teach?"

Larry noticed the eagerness in George's voice. "Hey, wait a minute! If you're thinking that this is something you can do, forget about it. It would take years of good behavior to allow you into a program like that. Anyhow, what would you teach? How to woo, dine, romance and then kill long-legged blue-eyed blonde women? Isn't that your talent?"

George gripped the bars on his cell, shut his eyes, and counted to ten. Now was not the time to retaliate; now was the time to think. If there was one thing he had on his side, it was time.

Remembering his next move made him smile. After months of attending a Bible study group, his repentant performance was glorious. There wasn't a dry eye in sight when he proclaimed himself a new man in Christ. Becoming an enthusiastic and intense Bible student had helped, and eventually his many years of good behavior made him the poster-boy for the case of social rehabilitation inside prisons. There were few doors closed to him when he felt that he knew enough about the Bible to start his own study group.

Larry. Never had he intended to harm Larry who had been the only guard in the system to join any Bible group, but he had joined George's. Believing that he was with his friend in Christ, Larry paid with his life for not checking the restraints on his prisoner. After George had waited years for such an opportunity, nothing was going to stop him, not even Larry. He waited until they were outside the gate before he slipped out of his restraints and, while trying to avoid Larry's unbelieving eyes, he killed him.

Driving while drinking is dangerous, and so is driving while having a panic attack. Everything had happened so fast he hadn't had time to think. It was when he realized that he had no idea what to do next, and it just a matter of time before someone noticed that the driver of the police van was wearing an orange suit, that reality struck.

He was still fighting for control of his emotions when a florist's truck suddenly shot in front of him. Driving is like riding a bike; once you know how, you never forget. But since he hadn't driven in ten years, his reactions were slow. Only the van's excellent brakes prevented a serious accident.

The driver of the truck never looked back at the skidding van behind him. Knowing that an accident right now would make his escape the shortest one in history, George's white-knuckled hands gripped the steering wheel in a wild effort to gain control. He was still breathing hard when the truck in front of him signaled a turn into the hospital's parking lot.

George followed.

Within minutes, the police van was ditched, his orange suit was covered by the florist's uniform with the name Dave stitched into the pocket, and dead Dave's body was covered with flowers in the back of the truck. In George's hand was the address for the next delivery. A

Laura Baker was going to get more than a floral bouquet when she answered the door. He needed a place to hide while he planned his next step, so with a little persuasion, this Laura woman was going to have company. He patted the pocket that held the gun he'd taken off Larry.

He had a solid plan until the long-legged blond lady jumped off the porch and ran to his truck. What a pleasant turn of events that had been.

Thinking about the woman jarred him completely awake. Opening his eyes, he saw what every prison inmate fantasizes about…a nude woman. But this wasn't fantasy, this was real.

Joan stood at the bottom of the bed and watched his beautiful package come to life. Playtime.

George's intention to open welcoming arms to her never happened.

He was tied to the bed.

# Chapter 24

Standing at the end of the dock, Josh looked into the clear water and wondered if today was the day. It wasn't the first morning that he'd stood here holding the can that contained Marie's ashes. Could he do it today? His breath caught in his throat, just knowing that if he emptied it, every trace of her would be gone forever.

He remembered the ceremony at the grave when the casket containing the shadow box and urn was buried. He was the only one who knew that the urn was empty. At the last minute, he'd grabbed an empty coffee can and poured her ashes into it. He wasn't ready to lose Marie then, and he wasn't ready to lose her now.

The empty feeling inside him that never gave him a moment's rest was like a black cloud that followed him when he walked into the cabin to place the can back on the fireplace mantel. Someday he had to do it because, even though they'd never discussed it, he just knew that's what Marie wanted. But not today.

The long empty hours stretched ahead of him with no hope that they would be different from any other day. He wasn't even pretending to write anymore. His publisher was calling for the return of the advance money he'd been paid for his next book. The deadline had come and gone days ago.

The urge to write was still strong. It was like a persistent itch that could only be relieved by his fingers pounding out a plot on the computer. Without Marie, what had once been so easy to do was now impossible.

Feeling out of sorts, he was on his way to the kitchen to make coffee when he remembered that along with many other items, he was out of it. Shopping had never been one of his jobs when they were here at the cabin. It was Marie's lists, not magic, that had filled the kitchen shelves. He used to tease her about her lists, but he wasn't laughing anymore. With a big sigh, he found paper and a pen and started one of his own.

Since he hadn't looked at himself in the mirror, he wasn't aware of the bags under his sleep-deprived eyes or the several days' growth of hair on his face. If his clothes looked as if he'd been sleeping in them, it was because he was. If he weren't able to sleep regularly, why bother putting on pajamas?

With the list in his pocket, Josh drove into town.

Even though it was late in the season, there were still enough visiting tourists and summer residents left in town to crowd the grocery store. He knew that when the season was completely over, this same store would be empty of shoppers. To stay in business year-round, all stores had to have a profitable summer in order to survive the long cold and snowy winter.

Pork chops or steak? Either one would be good cooked on the grill. Why not both? Having made up his mind, Josh was putting them into his cart when he smelled it. He froze. It was Marie's perfume.


Laura stepped back from the easel and studied her finished painting. It was the first one she'd done for Elizabeth, and as soon as the paint dried, she'd take it to A Spot of Color. It would take time for the money from Ben's life insurance policy to materialize, and until that happened, she was relying on the commission from the painting jobs to run her house.

Life without Ben was lonely. Toward the end, things hadn't been that good, but even thinking about why it hadn't been good only made her angry. The absence of the two people who had been important in her life had left a huge hole in her heart. She knew where Ben was because she'd seen him being lowered into the ground. And Joan? She hadn't seen her since she'd driven off with the florist guy, and she had no intention of spending any time wondering what that was all about. Joan was out of her life. Period.

A glance at the clock reassured her that she had time to deliver the painting and do some grocery shopping before the kids came home from school. They both had become clingy since their father's death. They'd sent the children off to camp with promises of seeing them soon, but Ben hadn't kept his promise. What assurance did they have that their mother wouldn't do the same thing? Ben's death had been hard on them.

She frowned, knowing that before the day was over, they both would be asking her questions about Aunt Joan. Where was she, and why hadn't she been to see them? They had so much to tell her about summer camp and their week with Grandma and Grandpa Baker. Laura was running out of excuses.

Leaving A Spot of Color with money in her purse, she went grocery shopping. While wheeling her cart through the checkout, she caught a glimpse of a man standing by the meat counter who looked almost familiar. Another look told her that she was mistaken. She didn't know any street people.

# Chapter 25

"What the hell?" George yelled.

"Shhhhh! It's a game!"

"Oh."

Joan giggled. "Is that all you have to say? Just 'oh'?"

He pulled on the ropes. "Think I'll wait until I hear the rules," he replied.

"There are no rules! You are mine and I can do whatever my little heart desires."

That got a grin out of him. "And then, will it be my turn to tie you up and do whatever my little heart desires?"

"Perhaps."

"What do you mean 'perhaps'?"

"Quit talking, and close your eyes."

Joan climbed into bed and straddled him.

His eyes might be shut, but George knew exactly what was happening.

Could life get any better than this?


Two hours later, he was exhausted.

"Really, Joan, I've had it. Time out."

"But I'm not tired."

"Let's rest a bit, okay?"

The look on her face bothered him. "The game isn't over until I say it's over."

"Well, I say it's over. No, no! Put down that vibrator, Joan! I have nothing more.... arg!"


George woke up to total darkness. Whatever had happened after the vibrator incident, he couldn't remember. His useless arms were numb, his penis felt raw, and he had to pee. He couldn't see, but he could feel some kind of cover over him.

If anyone could recognize crazy, it was he; the woman was insane.

An unbidden thought made him break out in a sweat. Hadn't one of Stephen King's scary stories been about someone being tied to a bed? The plot was hazy, but if he remembered correctly, it was a terrifying story.

It was the rush of adrenalin, ten years of workouts in the prison's gym, and abject fear that gave him the strength to break the rope on one arm. Within minutes, he was free and in the bathroom relieving himself.

Silently he prowled through the house looking for her. Now it was his turn; he was done playing by her rules. Ah, there she was, curled up on the sofa, sound asleep. Hopefully she'd stay asleep until he was ready, and then he'd wake her.

A search of the basement didn't provide him with everything he needed, but it was enough. Joan never stirred when George eased his arms under her, picked her up, and carried her to bed.

# Chapter 26

With a sigh of relief, Josh hung up the phone. The publisher had just granted him an extension with the understanding that if he didn't have the promised finished manuscript on his desk by the day of the deadline, Josh had to return the advance money.

Josh didn't have the money to return. It had been a hefty advance, but he'd used it to pay off expenses that Marie's medical insurance hadn't covered, and then the cost of her funeral wiped out any money that was left.

What was he to do? There was no story to write because his mind refused to cooperate with his typing fingers. And then there was the fact that writing under pressure had never worked for him. It was obvious; his writing days were over.

Deep in thought, he stepped to the window and looked out with unseeing eyes. What would happen when the deadline came and he had nothing to show his publisher? No manuscript and no advance money to return. Summer had turned into fall, and if he couldn't write, he might as well go home. Cold weather came early this far north and since the cabin wasn't insulated, the fireplace would be the only source of heat.

He was about to turn away from the window when his eyes landed on a canoe that was close to the shore. Was he getting company? He was reaching for the binoculars that he kept by the window for bird watching when a whiff of Marie's perfume startled him. Whirling around, he frantically scanned about the cabin hoping to catch sight of her. Nothing moved, and nothing was changed. Disappointed, he looked out the window again and saw the canoeist paddling toward the other side of the lake. There was something about the scene that caught his fancy. Slowly a plot formed in his head that ended with a devastated lover watching his beloved rowing away from him.

All thoughts of leaving the cabin fled. Words, sentences, paragraphs and chapters appeared in lightning speed as Josh pounded the keys on his computer. All his pent-up love, sorrow, and loss poured into his story while daylight fled and night turned into dawn.

It was late afternoon when Josh hit the send key and the manuscript was on its way to his publisher. He closed his computer, laid his head down on top of it, and fell instantly into welcome sleep.

Laura paddled away from the writer's cabin hoping he hadn't seen her. One of her commissioned jobs was on Green Lake, and once again she was back canoeing on the lake taking pictures of the subject with her new camera. Only this time she closely inspected the bottom of the canoe looking for patched leaks and she hadn't forgotten to wear a life jacket.

It was just morbid curiosity that lured her back into the area of her near-drowning scene. Surprised when she saw a car parked beside the writer's cabin, her first thought was to beach the canoe, knock on his door, and thank him properly for saving her life. What stopped her were the stories of how badly he treated visitors who interrupted his writing.

It was a good idea, but it wasn't worth taking a chance of upsetting Josh Lang who someday was going to autograph one of his books for her. Anyhow, she had to get back to her car and head home. It was going to be close, but unless she got stopped for speeding, she should make it before the kids got out of school.

She was having trouble concentrating because of a nagging concern for Joan. The feeling that something was wrong prompted her to call Joan's real estate office. They hadn't seen her either, but since she just worked when the mood struck, they weren't surprised.

What played in Laura's memory was the scene of Joan waving to her as the floral truck pulled away from the curb.

# Chapter 27

Joan woke up slowly, not wanting to disturb the memory of the beautiful man who had been in her dream…and then she remembered. Before she stretched out on the couch to rest, she'd tied the hunk to the bed to make sure he couldn't leave. Hopefully, he had a sense of humor. After all, it was just a game…a game that could, in the end, give her a beautiful baby.

Feeling a presence, she opened her eyes. The first thing she noticed was that she wasn't on the couch, the second thing she noticed was her beautiful plaything staring at her, and the third thing she noticed was that she couldn't move.

When tugging on the rope around her wrists didn't change anything, she attempted to sound unconcerned. "Come on, Dave, it's not your turn yet! Untie me!"

He just stared at her.

"What's the matter, Dave? I thought you were enjoying our little game!"

He didn't move.

"Dave, please?"

He spoke. "You can quit calling me Dave because that's not my name."

"Not your name? Then why did you tell me it was?"

"Because it was the name on the uniform I took off a guy named Dave who, by the way, is in the back of the truck covered with flowers. You know, the truck that's hidden in your garage right now?"

Joan started to shiver. "This Dave. Is he d..d..dead?"

"Very."

"Then, who are you?"

"Does the name George Knox ring a bell?"

Joan shook her head. And then fear filled her eyes.

"The serial killer? The polite gentleman who woos, dines, romances and then kills tall b..b..blond w..w..women?"

She had just described herself.

His grin was pure evil. "Nice of you to remember."

Her eyes went flying around the room, wildly searching for anything to get her out of the situation. That's when she saw what he had placed on the end table next to the bed.

She was going to die.

# Chapter 28

Determined to scatter Marie's ashes before he headed downstate, Josh stood on the edge of his dock holding the coffee can. The wind had picked up, making him wonder if this was a good time to scatter the ashes. He'd come up here to write a book, and he'd done that. With no more reason to stay, it was time to leave. Without Marie, maybe he'd just sell the cabin and all the memories that went with it.

Soon, there would be no trace of her left in this world. She had no family, except for him. Where she had come from, and how she ended up in foster care when she was a baby, was an unsolved mystery.

The story was that she'd been born after an accident that had killed both her parents. Whoever had delivered her had driven away with her, but later a guilty conscious had caused the person to abandon her on the steps of an adoption agency. Along with the blanket-wrapped baby, the abductor had left a note confessing to stealing the girl at the scene of a car crash. No amount of investigation turned up any case of a baby being stolen after an accident. Most of the social workers thought she was just another result of a teenage pregnancy, but Marie didn't. She had tried over the years to uncover more information, but back then the ability to gather and analyze DNA hadn't existed. That was the story in her records, and no one was ever able to verify or disclaim it.

With a sigh, he walked back toward the cabin where a plant bloomed with red roses and picked the biggest one he could find.

At the end of the dock, he said his final goodbye, and with his back to the wind, scattered the ashes, tossed the rose, and watched as the wind-driven waves pushed them on their journey.

It was time to head back downstate.

On the other side of the lake, Laura was hurriedly packing up her easel and collecting her painting supplies. The day had started out so nice, she'd decided to finish the painting at the actual site and not just from a picture she'd taken of the cabin, but the wind was picking up and dark clouds were moving in.

With everything stowed in her car, she took one last walk on the dock that stretched out into the water just to watch the wave activity. A clap of thunder startled her. It had been an enjoyable early fall day on a beautiful lake, but it was time to go.

As she turned to leave, a high wave washed over the dock, depositing something at her feet as it retreated. Bending down, she picked up a beautiful red rose.


The next morning, the one red rose that graced the table almost looked out of place in the midst of the breakfast remains. Teddy and Beth's half-eaten bowls of oatmeal were turning into cement while the remains of a spilled glass of orange juice was puddling under a soggy piece of toast.

Lying beside her cup of cold coffee were several days of the morning paper that she hadn't even glanced at. Without Ben, the backbone of the day's structure was gone. No more elaborate dinners to cook, and now there was no one to say that she couldn't work outside the home. For some reason, freedom wasn't feeling very free.

With a huge sigh, she gathered the pile of newspapers, took them to the trashcan in the garage, and tossed them in. She just wasn't in the mood to read old news.

It was just the first week of the new school year, and according to the note that he'd reluctantly handed her, Teddy's teacher wanted to talk to her today during the lunch break. Both Teddy and Beth ate lunch at the school's cafeteria, so that wasn't a problem. Was Miss Nelson going to tell her that Teddy was misbehaving? He had taken Ben's death really hard.

After cleaning up from breakfast, there would be time to finish the second commissioned painting for A Touch of Color before she had to leave for the conference. The insurance benefits still hadn't materialized and she needed the money.

Her surprise at the low balance in their joint accounts had been explained when she'd found Ben's hidden statements from another bank. The son-of-a-bitch had been transferring money from their joint account to ones with only his name on it.

Her surprise turned into anger when she'd arrived at the bank with the statements and the bank officials informed her that since her name was not on the accounts, she had no right to the money. No right to the money? Of course she had a right to the money! "Talk to your lawyer," was their reply.

Laura had left the bank with steam coming out of her ears. Her one wish was that Ben was still alive so that she could have the pleasure of killing him herself.

# Chapter 29

How could she have a conference with a parent when all she wanted to do was to sit in the dark and cry?

Dave's employer was saying awful things about her fiancé, threatening what he was going to do if his flower truck wasn't returned immediately. Dave and his truck just seemed to have disappeared. It hadn't helped that every agency in town had the license plate and description of it. Had Dave fled town?

The thought brought on fresh tears. He loved her! Her mind refused to consider that maybe they had been a bit hasty in announcing their engagement. Was making a commitment enough reason for him to run?

With one last touch of powder to her red nose, she left the lounge to return to her classroom where she had been told Teddy's mother was waiting for her.


Laura was getting impatient. It was past the noon hour and Miss Nelson wasn't anywhere to be seen. With time on her hands, she walked around the room and inspected the pictures displayed on the bulletin board. Teddy's stuck out not only because it was colorful, it also showed some drawing talent. Maybe she'd passed her artistic genes on to him. Could that be what Miss Nelson wanted to talk to her about?

"Good afternoon, Mrs. Baker. Thank you for coming, and I apologize for being late."

At the sound of Miss Nelson's voice, Laura turned around expecting to see the excited face of the pretty young teacher she'd met before. What she saw alarmed her.

"Miss Nelson! Are you ill?"

"No, no! I'm not ill, Mrs. Baker. Please have a seat."

Tall Laura had trouble fitting into the child-sized desk; petite Miss Nelson had no problem.

"There are a couple of things about Theodore that I need to talk to you about." Holding herself rigid, she was determined to get through the conference without crying. "I hope you noticed Teddy's picture on the bulletin board. He is sh...sh...owing, ah, he is sh...." That's as far as she got before she burst into tears.

Laura had no idea what to do. Do you dare take your kid's teacher into your arms and comfort her?

With her face buried in a tissue, Miss Nelson exclaimed, "I'm so sorry. I thought I could do this, but I can't. Thank you for coming, but you'll have to leave."

"Miss Nelson, obviously there's something terribly wrong. I have no intention of prying into why you are so troubled, but is there anything I can do?"

Miss Nelson shook her head. "Not unless you can tell me where my fiancé and his flower truck are. Seems like they both disappeared off the face of the earth. But you must have read all about it in the paper. It's been front page news."

A flash memory of Joan crawling into the passenger side of a floral truck made Laura catch her breath.

Laura was counting back the days to the last time she'd seen Joan. It was before the funeral that a friend who couldn't make it had sent flowers and a note to apologize for not being able to attend. Should she say something?

Laura was still pondering what to do when she noticed that Miss Nelson was running out of the room.

Laura went home.

A quick trip to the garage, and Laura returned to the kitchen with the few issues of the paper that had escaped the breakfast coffee grounds. Spreading the readable ones on the kitchen table, she looked for anything that pertained to the missing truck. Her heart skipped a beat when she found an enlarged photo of the driver. It was a picture of a clean-cut young man whose face she'd never seen before. And she *had* seen the driver of the truck when she'd looked out her window to see who was ringing her doorbell; it sure wasn't the face in the paper.

So, who was driving the truck that Joan had crawled into?

The answer to that question was on a coffee-soaked front page of one of the papers that hadn't made it to the kitchen table.

# Chapter 30

Sounds of George mumbling to himself along with the slamming shut of kitchen drawers roused Joan from her semi-conscious state. Her nose couldn't detect the smell of cooking, so what was he doing in her kitchen?

Poor George was in a raging fit because he hadn't been able to replicate all of his torture instruments from the paltry offerings in John's basement workshop. The tension that constantly built up inside of him was sated only if he followed a set torture routine, and the last thing before he killed them, he *had* to tattoo his last name onto their forehead. Only then would the darkness leave his soul. His problem now was that he didn't have the right equipment to do the job; a carpenter's nail was the closest thing he could find that would produce the same tattoo result.

He had no idea what he was looking for, but if there was anything in the kitchen that would help, he knew he would recognize it when he saw it. And there, hanging on a hook by the oven, was a potholder. That should work. While he held the carpenter's nail over the gas stove's flame, his fingers wouldn't get burned if he had them inside the potholder.

Joan had drifted off when a harsh cry filled with profanity came from the kitchen and the strong smell of something burning woke her. She lay in her own filth, her arms numb from being tied to the bed, her throat raw from screaming, and wondered what torture he was planning. The serial killer, who had been the scourge of the country ten years ago, was known for his ritualistic treatment of his victims. From remembering old accounts, Joan knew that he didn't kill the women right away. Oh, they all ended up dead, but before that happened, he made sure his mark was on them. If she hadn't been so scared, it might have been funny that the ruckus coming from the kitchen sounded like the screams of a little girl.

Joan was resigned to die. John wouldn't be home until the weekend, and Laura wasn't her friend anymore. She had nothing going on at work that would make anyone try to get in contact with her. Tears slipped out of her eyes when reality hit; no one was going to rescue her.

What she didn't notice when George rushed into the room with his hand inside a potholder carrying a red-hot nail was that both his eyebrows were singed.

Joan's screams were music to his ears. Stepping back from the bed, he viewed his artwork. The hot nail worked, but it was only good for three or four marks before it stopped burning the flesh on her forehead. The first letter of his last name looked shaky, but it definitely was a K. It certainly wasn't his finest work, but without the proper equipment, it was the best he could do.

Joan had passed out.


Laura drove slowly past Joan's house. There was no car in her driveway, but there wouldn't have to be one even if John were home, which she doubted. Their three-car garage had always been a source of envy for Ben.

Joan might not be her friend anymore, but old habits die hard. If she could just peek inside the garage to make sure the Bentley was there, maybe she could stop worrying. And then Laura remembered that Joan hadn't driven her car on the day of their break-up; she'd walked. Seeing her car in the garage wouldn't tell her anything.

Still, the feeling that something wasn't right wouldn't go away. Stopping her car halfway down the block, she crawled out and headed for the back of Joan's wooded property. Just one peek through the master bedroom window was all she wanted. It would be easy enough because the big windowed access door to the small deck John had built at the back of the house was in their bedroom. On weekends when he was home, that's where you'd find the two of them enjoying the peaceful view and a cup of coffee. Just one peek was all she wanted, and then she'd forget about it.

She was cutting through the neighbor's back yard when the sound of growling stopped her. Standing as quietly as she could, she watched as a large reddish-tan-colored dog advanced toward her, snarling as it stalked. Oh, God! What are you supposed to do when a dog is about to attack? Do you look into its eyes? No, that's not right. Do you talk to it?

"Nice d..d..doggy!"

"Uh, sit? Please sit!"

"Go home!"

Nothing was working. She did remember that she shouldn't run, but that's exactly what she wanted to do.

And then from one of the houses she heard, "Rusty, dinner time!"

The dog's ears went up, he whirled around and then to her relief, he ran toward the sound of the voice.

On shaky legs, she made it back to the car where she sat behind the wheel until her pounding heart settled down. A glance at the clock on the car's dashboard told her it was almost time for Beth and Teddy's bus to drop them off. All thoughts of Joan and the dog were replaced by the need to be home waiting with milk and cookies when the kids walked into the house.

# Chapter 31

Home was not home without Marie. Unable to sleep in their bed, the couch became Josh's refuge at night. But sleep was not easy. Every time he closed his eyes, cruel reality hit; death was final. Between grief and the strong urge to drive back to the cabin, most nights found him wide awake staring at the ceiling. He had just gotten back from the lake, so what was making him think he should return? Could it be that Marie was upset with him for leaving the cabin in such a mess?

His manuscript had been edited, and of all the others he'd written, this one needed the least rewriting of any of them. The words that his fingers had pounded out on the computer in the short period of time had been spot on. The same artist who had created the cover for all his other books was working on the one that was scheduled to come out around Christmas.

Not having a deadline hanging over him was a relief but in a way, he missed it. The threat of having to return the advance if he didn't produce had at least given him a reason to get out of bed in the morning.

And then, there was the thought that without Marie, why should he hang onto the cabin? Going there was nothing more than opening himself up for more pain. God, how he missed her! Why not put it on the market?

It was a spur-of-the-moment decision. A quick call to the realtor who specialized in lake property in the cabin's area, some clean clothes thrown into a case, and with the keys in his hand, he headed for his car.

The first sight of the beautiful little lake usually gave Josh a feeling of contentment; today it wasn't happening. As he got closer he could see that there was another car already there, probably the real estate agent. Damn! He'd intended to get rid of the beer bottles and clean up a bit before she arrived. And his bed. Had he left it unmade? Marie would be so upset and even embarrassed for anyone to see the cabin in such a state.

An hour later, the real estate agent drove away from Josh Lang's cabin with mixed feelings. The cabin would have been so easy to sell! It was the first time in her long career that she'd actually talked a seller out of putting his property on the market. Grief-stricken Josh was not ready for such a drastic step. Later, if he still wanted to sell, she was sure he'd contact her.

What she did have in her trunk were several outfits from his wife's closet and some new ones that still had the price tags on them. While walking with him through the cabin suggesting things he would want to do if he really were going to put his property on the market, she pointed to their limited closet space that presently was crowded with mostly his deceased wife's clothing. Since the realtor's family owned the resale store in town, she offered to help him with the crowded closet problem.

It was hard for him to pick out dresses and a coat or two that he'd seen her wear, but he did. It was easier to choose the new ones that still had the price tag on them. He had bought them himself in an effort to cheer Marie up when the routine of three-times-a-week dialysis became wearisome and they'd fled to the lake hoping that she would be well enough to attend holiday parties with their neighbors. He just wasn't ready to part with everything. That's all he had left of her.

# Chapter 32

Joan drifted between actual terror and nightmare horror, sometimes not bothering to figure out which one it was. What surprised her was how much she longed for death for there would be nothing worth living for after George was through with her. Her forehead burned like the fire of Hell, and since her tied hands were stretched out above her head, she really didn't know how many of the throbbing fingers had lost their nails. Frustrated over the slow progress of burning his name into her forehead, he'd been venting his anger by removing them.

What day was it? She had no idea. John was supposed to return home Friday night, Saturday morning at the latest. By that time, she was sure George would be long gone, and John would walk into the house wondering where the awful smell was coming from. When he arrived at the source, he'd find his mutilated dead wife lying in her own filth. Poor John. He and Ben had been such good friends, but since Ben was dead, would he turn to Laura for comfort?

The sounds of muttering, cussing and the yelp from what was probably a burned finger coming from the kitchen woke her from a troubled sleep.

George was heating the nail, again.


Laura walked the kids to the bus stop and then waved to them as it drove away. A long day ahead with no demands hanging over her, there was an empty feeling inside her. She missed Ben and Joan.

It wasn't that she didn't have things to do today, because she had. Since she was running short on money, she would finish the second commissioned painting from A Spot of Color and then take it to Elizabeth. If she could believe what she was being told, the life insurance money might be slow in coming, but it was coming. She had contacted a lawyer about Ben's two bank accounts, however his talk of wills and probate court was too much to take in right now. "Just fix it," she'd told him. "I need the money."

The morning went fast. For nine years, she'd forgotten how much fun it was to create a canvas that seemed to come alive under the magic of her brush. By lunchtime, the canvas was finished and drying while Laura cleared up her painting area.

How her life had changed! Ben would have had a fit with the casual way she was now keeping house. Life with him hadn't been easy. Raising two kids while trying to keep the house looking as if no children lived there was almost impossible. The frantic activity to remove any evidence of their day occurred after Ben's call from work saying he was on his way home. When he arrived, the house would be pristine, and both kids would be in their rooms so that Ben wouldn't be disturbed while he drank the martini Laura handed to him as he walked in the door.

She hated to admit it, but she and the children seemed much more relaxed since he was gone.

As she backed out of her driveway for the short drive to A Spot of Color, the urge to check on Joan's house was impossible to ignore. Nothing more than a slow drive-by, she promised herself. Joan was probably there, safe and sound with a funny story to share about how she'd surprised the driver of the floral truck by asking him to give her a ride home. God, she missed Joan and her antics almost more than she missed Ben.

The morning paper! That's what she'd look for. If there was a pile of papers by her front door, then she'd know that Joan wasn't home. Then she could really worry about her old friend.

A slow drive past Joan's house showed no activity inside. No lights were on, but she must be home because there were no newspapers on her doorstep.

# Chapter 33

George Knox was having fun reading the newspaper stories about the unsuccessful manhunt. What a neat situation the woman Joan had handed him on a silver platter: a garage to hide the truck, a place to stay, food to eat, and clothes to wear. The husband's side of the walk-in closet was full of casual clothes that fit him perfectly. There was enough money just laying around inside drawers and in Joan's purse to tide him over until he figured out his next step.

Knowing Joan's husband was due home at the end of the week, George was well aware that he had to finish the job he'd started on Joan soon and then when he left, he'd be driving her red Bentley. What an exit this was going to be! The only thing left to do was finish one leg of the x on the last letter of his name. Just one more session with the nail, and then he'd kill her.

Now, where was the damn potholder? When a quick search of the kitchen didn't produce it, he finally remembered that he'd left it on the table by Joan's bed. No problem. He'd just wrap his hand with a kitchen towel.

He actually hummed while the nail heated up. Where would he go? The chance of his finding another situation as good as this one was slim. According to the newspaper, the search for him was nationwide, but after Joan's body was found, they'd know he was still in the area. It was going to be fun driving away in the Bentley, but he'd have to ditch it almost immediately. At least now he had clothes and money, but with no idea where to go or what to do, the truth hit hard. He stopped humming.

He was going to get caught.

His hand jerked and the loosely wrapped towel slipped toward the flames. The next few seconds were filled with girlish screams as flames from the burning towel quickly spread to the sleeve of his borrowed jacket. Off came the burning items, and with a wild throw in the direction of the sink, they flew through the air…straight into the kitchen curtains. If Joan hadn't been unconscious, she would have heard an unearthly scream, followed by the smell of something burning.

The house was on fire.

A contented and happy Laura with money in her pocket was on her way home after a lovely afternoon spent in A Spot of Color visiting with other local artists. It was as if the nine-year absence had never happened.

Old habits are hard to break, and while driving home, she turned onto Joan's street just to drive past her house. What she had done was unforgivable and they never could be friends again, but Laura missed the fun-loving and exuberant Joan. No one had seen or heard from her recently, and Laura couldn't help but worry. In her mind's eye, she kept seeing Joan driving away in the florist's truck. She stopped the car when she noticed that the garage door was opening, making Laura feel disgusted with herself. She had wasted all that energy worrying about Joan and here she'd been home this whole time.

Too late, she became aware that the Bentley was roaring down the driveway straight at her car. Before she closed her eyes to brace herself for the impact, she got a glimpse of the driver; it sure wasn't Joan. The car skidded past her with just inches to spare.

It was then that she saw smoke billowing out of the house. It just took a few seconds for all the animosity and bitterness towards Joan to flee. Her friend was in trouble. A quick call to 911 brought the fire department, and in a matter of minutes the front door was battered down. A frantic Laura didn't let the shouts of "Lady, get back here!" slow her down.

The house was quickly filling with black smoke, but she didn't stop her search until she found her friend.

# Chapter 34

Laura sat beside the hospital bed and quietly talked to Joan whose dull eyes were just staring off into space. She had an urge to touch her, to reassure her that now she was safe, but one glance at Joan's blistered forehead and heavily bandaged hands discouraged the urge.

"Joan, can you hear me? It's me, Laura. You know, your best friend since grade school? Come on, Joan, blink your eyes if you can hear me. Okay, that didn't work. Maybe you think I'm still angry about what you did with my husband. I must admit that I was pretty steamed up about that, but I'm willing to forgive you if you'd just blink your eyes. Just once."

Nothing.

Laura was near tears. "Ah, Joanie, don't shut me out, please! You have to recognize my voice!"

A hand fell on her shoulder and made her whirl around to find a well-dressed man standing behind her.

"You must be Laura," he smiled. "Horrible circumstances, but it's good to finally run into you. I needed a face to go along with all the stories I've heard about you!"

Laura's mouth opened in alarm.

"Oh, I guess I should introduce myself. I'm Dr. Zumwalt, Joan's psychiatrist."

Laura relaxed. "She talked about me?"

"All the time."

"Then you know about her and my husband?"

He nodded.

She hesitated before she asked, "I know you can't talk about it, but she was shocked because I didn't understand why she had to get involved with my Ben."

"Laura, all I can say is that it seemed perfectly rational to her. At the end, I discovered that she was holding back information that would have helped me understand how deep her desire was to have a baby. She didn't tell me things because, in her own words, she didn't want me to think she was crazy."

Laura shook her head. "What a waste! Will she ever be her old self again?"

Dr. Zumwalt thought for a moment before he answered quietly. "Maybe she never wants to be her old self again. To do that, she'd have to relive everything that evil man did to her."

Laura sighed and reaching down, she brushed Joan's hair off her face.

"It would take intense therapeutic sessions, but it could be done," Dr. Zumwalt added.

Laura sighed again. "That would be a painful thing to ask her to do, but I just miss her so much!"

Dr. Zumwalt patted her shoulder. "Speaking of the evil man, is there any word about finding him?"

"Nothing. He ditched the Bentley almost immediately in the long-term parking area at the airport. The owner of the car that he hot-wired must have left the parking card inside the car, because George was able to check out of the lot with no trouble. The owner could be gone for days or weeks before he comes home and finds his car is gone."

The psychiatrist sighed. "So, George Knox is out there, probably looking for another tall, blond woman. Since he didn't get to kill Joan, his frustration level must be fairly high."

"Is that how his sickness works?"

Dr. Zumwalt shrugged. "I remember studying about Knox while I was still at the University. He's very good at hiding the evil inside of him. It appears he is quite a charming man who is able to live a relatively normal life, except the urge to kill tall blond women is always simmering under the surface, building up steam. There were chapters in our textbooks that were written by the prison psychiatrist. None of them could find the source that would explain George's behavior." He pointed to Joan. "That's how he relieves the pent-up steam."

"So, it's your belief that since he didn't finish the job with Joan, he's out there looking for another victim?"

Dr. Zumwalt studied Laura. "You do know that you fit that description, don't you?"

Laura nodded. "Makes me want to change the color of my hair."

"Wouldn't hurt," was the doctor's solemn answer.

"I'm not going to worry about George Knox!" Laura replied. "It would be dumb of him to hang around this part of the country while every agency is on the lookout for him. He's hundreds of miles away by now."

"You're probably right," the doctor agreed. "Oh, by the way, where is Joan's husband?"

"His job has him traveling all week, usually returning home either Friday evening or early Saturday morning. Since no one knows how to get in contact with him except Joan, I do believe someone should hang around until he does come home. Finding his house burned and a tortured wife who probably won't recognize him is going to be a shocker."

Dr. Zumwalt glanced at the unconscious Joan.

"I'll do it," he offered.

# Chapter 35

Josh stood with his back to the blazing fireplace and savored the heat that was slowly warming him after his time outside splitting logs. An early cold spell had hit the area just as he'd finished insulating the cabin, but even with keeping the fireplace burning around the clock, it wasn't enough.

In his grieving state of mind, he hadn't considered what it would be like to live in a cabin where the only amenities were running water and electricity. Since they'd only used it in the summer, there was no need for insulation or a heating system.

His decision to return to the lake had been made in haste and the items he'd thrown into his car had not included warm clothing. As soon as he warmed up, he was heading into town to find the solution to his heating problem and while he was there, he'd shop; the first item on the list to buy was a pair of long johns.

One hour later he was walking out of the only plumbing and heating store in town feeling a lot better about his cold cabin. It was going to be expensive, but electric baseboard heat was the solution to his problem. By the end of the week, the cabin would have a heat source to add to the warmth from the fireplace. Glancing at the new calluses on his hands from splitting logs, he was imagining how impressive they were going to be by the end of winter.

He and Marie had never shopped for clothes while staying at the cabin, so he had no idea which way to turn when he left the heating store. He walked slowly, pausing whenever something in the window attracted him. It was when he was strolling by a resale store that a whiff of Marie's perfume froze him. His frantic eyes searching for the source of the scent landed on the mannequin in the store's window; she was wearing one of Marie's dresses.

His mind whirled and his heart pounded until he remembered giving a few of Marie's clothes to the realtor for her family's shop.

He was about to continue on when a curious thought hit him. The original price tag was still on it, so Marie had never worn the dress.

His casual stroll quickened as he put distance between him and the shop. He was much too sensible to be allowing these unusual circumstances to affect him. There had to be a rational explanation for the shadow box, the song, the perfume...the dress.

Or maybe he was losing his mind?


Laura left the hospital with a heavy heart. Joan's body might live, but the woman inside had changed. George Knox had turned her friend into someone she didn't recognize, both physically and mentally.

How often had she envied Joan for having her freedom unfettered by motherhood? All the while, Joan was suffering because she wasn't fettered by motherhood. According to Dr. Zumwalt, Joan's need to become a mother was intense enough to force her into unhealthy situations.

With her head full of memories, she walked through the center of town. Her thoughts went to the last time she and Joan had texted. Pulling out her iPhone, she looked up their last message.

Joan: *Hey, girlfriend, been missing you. Coffee?*

Laura: *Busy. I'm painting again.*

Joan: *Good for you! I always wondered why you quit.*

Laura: *Ha. Spoken like someone who has never had kids!*

Joan: *Don't rub it in, girlfriend! I'm still trying.*

Laura put away the phone and used her coat sleeve to wipe away the tears that were running down her cheeks. How insensitive of her to mention that she had kids and Joan had none. As close as they were, she had hidden her misery well.

Joan's dead eyes and mutilated face kept popping up unbidden in Laura's mind. Her friend, who was always beautifully dressed, would hate it if she knew she was wearing a drab hospital gown. What she needed was a colorful bed jacket.

With that thought in mind, Laura's aimless stroll turned into one with purpose. Across the street, she spied the window of a resale shop that had a mannequin dressed in a beautiful outfit. When the traffic cleared, she crossed the street heading for the door.

"Good afternoon!" the sales person greeted her.

"Good afternoon to you, too!" Laura answered.

"Looking for something in particular?"

"Yes, I am, but it was the dress in the window that lured me in."

The salesperson smiled. "Yes, it is beautiful. It's brand new. Has never been worn."

"I can see that." The original price had been crossed out, but even at a discount, the dress was still quite expensive. "However, it's a bit out of my price range."

"Could I show you several others that came from the same source? They have been worn and are less expensive."

"I suppose I could look, but a dress is not what I'm shopping for. Oh," she cried when she spotted a coat that she liked. "Could I try that one on?"

"Certainly! The dressing rooms are to your right."

Laura stood in the dressing room gazing at herself in the mirror. The coat fit her as if were made especially for her. She stepped out of the dressing room, walked to the front of the store and was showing the saleslady how she looked in the coat when she saw a man standing outside the shop staring intently at the mannequin.

Laura's breath caught in her throat. "Isn't that Josh Lang, the writer?" she asked.

The saleslady nodded. "I hear that his wife died recently."

"Yes, I heard that, too," Laura replied.

"Poor man."

"One of these days he's going to autograph one of his books for me," Laura announced.

The saleslady's face lit up. "Oh, I already have two of his that he autographed! He really is a friendly man, except when he's writing."

Laura laughed. "Someone told me about that. But he did something for me that's much better than autographing my book."

"And what was that?"

"He saved me from drowning."

"No!"

"Yes!"

"So, you know him quite well?"

Laura shook her head. "When he got me to shore, he just dumped me and said he hoped I had my own transportation home."

"Well, I suspect that he'll be more approachable the next time you see him."

"If there is a next time," Laura mused.

"I hear he's fixing up the cabin so that he can spend the winter at the lake."

"Is that so?"

"There are a lot of parties around the holidays. Maybe you'll run into him again at one of them."

"I'd like that because I never got to really thank him for saving me. I'll have to wander around with one of his books in my bag!"

The saleslady studied Laura. "Please tell me you're going to buy that coat. It looks like it was just waiting for you."

"Yes, I am going to buy it. But what I'm really looking for is a bed jacket. A good friend of mine needs something pretty right now. Do you have any?"

"Indeed I do! Several of them came in with the coats and dresses. I think you're going to have trouble picking just one because they are all beautiful."

# Chapter 36

This was freedom?

With his thin jacket pulled up over his face, George's breath was the only source of heat in the car. Even this far north, the drop in temperature was unusually early this year. If it weren't for the fact that he needed every drop of gas in his tank for a quick get-away, he'd just start the car and let the heater warm him. The coating on his un-brushed teeth was disgusting and with his face under his jacket, he could smell his unwashed body.

It was getting light outside, and he knew without even looking that a rat the size of a kitten would be watching him, his whiskers would be twitching and his nose would be pushed up against the windshield. His visits were so frequent George had named him.

His idea to park his car in the junkyard at night while he slept was a good one. He hadn't seen any wanted posters in town, but that didn't mean there weren't any. It wasn't too often that a serial killer escaped and remained at large for this length of time.

He could only imagine what was going on back at his old prison. Finding that the reformed lady-killer really hadn't been reformed had to have knocked the wind out of the prison's rehabilitation program. News of what he'd done to Joan would prove that the idea didn't work.

His life had been reduced to sleeping in his car, buying food from a fast-food drive through hoping no one would look at him too closely, and his only companion was Roger the Rat.

His fast exit from Joan's burning house had left him with just the clothes on his back and the wad of bills he'd found under the panties in Joan's drawer. Whatever it was that she'd been squirreling money for had to be something really big. He had to start taking chances. He didn't know what he was looking for, but he knew he'd recognize an opportunity when he saw it. The money wouldn't last forever, and before it ran out, he had to find a way to survive outside prison.

Roger the Rat watched George when he got out of the car to relieve himself. It was only after he was startled by the sound of the car starting that he jumped off the hood.

George drove to the fast-food restaurant where the smell of bacon made his stomach growl for a lot more than a cup of coffee and a sweet roll. Driving was dangerous. He knew that there were cops out there who would love to be the one who nabbed the number one guy on the Most Wanted list.

He slowed down and took a long look at a seedy looking motel just outside town. The thought of a real bed and a hot shower made him salivate. In the past, his charm and good looks had gotten him through a lot of bad situations, but right now he looked and smelled like a bum. He needed to get cleaned up, and to stay out of prison, he had to change his appearance

Ever since the fight in prison had left him with a chipped front tooth, he never smiled when he looked at himself in the mirror. Before his fake conversion, a good part of his time had been spent in isolation for fighting. He'd forgotten the inmate's name who'd done it, but he'd bet the inmate hadn't forgotten his. The guy had ended up with a long stay in the prison's infirmary, and George spent a long time in solitary confinement.

So, he wasn't smiling when he looked at his reflection in his rearview mirror. What he saw was a good-looking man with a head of thick black hair, albeit greasy, and the beginning of a dark beard. He could change the color of his hair, but then it wouldn't match the daily growth on his face. He'd always been vain about his hair, but it had to go.

It took a stop at the drugstore to buy supplies and a short stay at the motel in order to rest and change his appearance. He also had to come up with a generic name that would be so ordinary that no one would pay attention.


Roger the Rat watched a different-looking man who was now calling himself Bob Miller walk out of the junkyard. In case the stolen car was spotted before he needed it again, he'd carefully removed any trace of himself with an alcohol-soaked rag.

# Chapter 37

The first thing Laura saw when she stepped out of the resale shop with a package under her arm was an unfamiliar tall baldheaded man across the street who was staring in her direction. Laura glanced around, not seeing anyone else in her vicinity so she assumed he was new in town. She smiled and waved at him, knowing that her small town had a habit of being overly welcoming. Even from across the street she could see the pleased look on his face when he waved back.

All thoughts of the stranger disappeared when she saw a slumped-shoulders, dejected looking man walking toward her.

"Hello, John," she called out to Joan's husband.

His head jerked up, and for a second, his eyes were unfocused. "Oh, it's you, Laura." He blinked a few times before he really looked at her.

They'd been close friends for a long time, but how do you talk to someone who had come home from a business trip to find his wife beaten and his house burned? She felt that if she were empathetic, he'd burst into tears right here on the sidewalk, so she said the first thing that came into her head.

"Yes, it's me. I just bought Joan some pretty bed jackets."

"That's nice," he mumbled, and kept walking.

"John?" she called.

He didn't stop, even when he ran full force into the tall baldheaded man who had just crossed from the other side of the street.

Struggling to regain his balance, the man barked, "Watch where you're going!"

"Sorry," John replied without raising his head.

When John continued to walk away, the stranger looked at Laura and shrugged.

"You'll have to excuse his rudeness," Laura explained. "The poor man has reason to be distracted."

George Knox smiled at her, took an interested look at the leggy blond, but kept walking. He'd keep her in mind, but he had no intention of getting involved in his favorite activity until he was finished with Joan.

His walk through town looking for opportunities had taken him past a big white Colonial home that had a bed and breakfast sign in the yard, and in the back, he could see a row of cabins that bordered a heavily wooded area. Resting against the handle of a rake, a small dark-haired woman wiped the sweat off her forehead, smiled and waved to him. For his whole adult life, women had been attracted to him, but since his body only responded to tall blonds, he had no interest following up on the greeting.

An hour later he was exhausted and out of ideas. Except for the bed and breakfast, he was disappointed that the walk through town had not generated any other possibilities.

The woman was still struggling to rake leaves off the driveway when George returned.

"Good afternoon, ma'am," he called out.

She stopped raking and turned to look at the able-bodied man trying to get her attention.

"May I help you, sir?"

"Could I have a word with you?"

She nodded. "If you don't call me ma'am, you may. You're making me feel like my mother."

Trying to look apologetic, he bowed his head. "Sorry about that."

She dropped the rake and walked over to him. "What can I do for you?"

George kept his eyes on the ground, trying to appear embarrassed for what he was about to ask. "First, I'll tell you my problem," he said, finally raising his eyes to look into hers. "I was just passing through your town when my car conked out. I was told it would be some time before the parts came in, and since I had to pay for them upfront, I'm stuck in your lovely town with no money and no car."

"Sir, I'm really sorry for your troubles. How can I help?"

"Well, I could help you."

"Help me?" Her eyebrows rose in question. "Help me do what?"

He tilted his head and turned on the charm. "For one thing, I could finish the leaf-raking job."

She took one look at the vast area that still needed to be cleared of colorful leaves and her eyes lit up with interest. "Go on."

"I'm also quite handy with tools, and I'm strong. I could do your maintenance, and even help with housekeeping."

Nancy was trying to keep her excitement from showing. Mike had been gone for almost a year and repair jobs were piling up. "And what would you want in return?"

"Nothing much. Just someplace to sleep and food to eat until my car gets fixed. I promise you won't be sorry."

"No money involved?"

"No money. Oh, maybe just a few dollars to put gas in my car when it gets fixed so that I can get on with my trip."

Ever since Mike's untimely death, Nancy had been struggling to keep the door to her business open. Lack of customers wasn't the problem; it was the physical work of cooking, cleaning, changing beds, laundry, and maintenance that kept her constantly exhausted. There just weren't enough hours in the day for one person to stay on top of it all.

She took a good look at the tall baldheaded man whose smile was revealing teeth that looked especially white in contrast to the black growth on his face. The chipped front one gave him a devilish look that added to his charisma. This man just might mean the difference between keeping her business going and closing its doors.

The decision made, she remarked, "We really should exchange names before we start making plans. My name is Nancy Blair."

George's mind went blank for a second before the new name popped into his head. "My name is Bob, Bob Miller."

"Glad to meet you, Bob. Now we can get down to business. Are you picky about your living conditions?"

"Are you asking if I want a room in your home or stay in one of your cabins? Then the answer is that I will accept whatever you have to offer."

She pointed at a shed way in the back of the property. "When my husband and I bought this place, we found a room in there that has

96

a bed, a dresser, and a space heater in it. It doesn't have a bathroom, so you'd be welcome to use the one in the house. Since we've never used the room, it would have to be cleaned. Would that work?"

Husband? He'd never thought of a husband.

"Is your husband around? You probably should talk to him before we go any further," George commented.

"I lost Mike a year ago, so no, there's no husband around. If there were, I wouldn't need your help."

George heaved a sigh of relief. He could hide out here for as long as he needed. Visions of the tall blond woman he'd seen earlier today flashed into his mind.

The isolated shed would be perfect.

# Chapter 38

"Joan, help me!" Laura pleaded. Trying to get the bed jacket on Joan's limp body was a struggle she hadn't anticipated. "You're going to like this one. It's really pretty."

Even though Joan had yet to respond to any outside stimulation, Laura wanted to believe that she could hear her. "It's a beautiful day!" she continued. "I left my car at home this morning and I've been walking, enjoying the fall sunshine. Nothing much is going on in town to talk about. Oh, I saw your John on the way here. He wasn't looking where he was going and he ran smack into a man I'd never seen before. Almost knocked him off his feet!"

Joan's body stiffened.

"Oh, you didn't like my story?"

Joan's body didn't change.

"You want to talk about John?"

She remained stiff.

"Is it the stranger you want to hear about?"

Joan slumped.

"Okay, he was tall, had the beginnings of a black beard, and I guess he'd have black hair if he had any, but he didn't. He was completely bald."

Joan body stiffened.

"Wrong stranger?"

No response.

Laura finished tying the bow at the neckline of the jacket. "Now, don't you look pretty!" she lied. Joan looked anything but pretty.

"Well, I'm going to go now, but I'll be back tomorrow." Picking up Joan's limp hand, she squeezed it. "Can you feel that?"

No response.

"I know you can hear me because you reacted when I mentioned seeing a stranger, but when I described the one I saw, you did nothing. Was that because my description didn't fit the one you had in mind? Is that right?"

No response.

Laura knew that George Knox was Joan's attacker, and from the Most Wanted posters, everyone knew what he looked like. Had Joan thought the stranger might be George? Couldn't be. He was too smart to stay in the town where Joan lived and where everyone was looking for him.

Laura headed to the front desk to report that she'd gotten a weak response from Joan when she mentioned the stranger, but when no one was there, she tucked it away to tell them later.

The day that had started out sunny was threatening to turn into something else. The blue sky had darkened and black clouds were racing to cover the sun by the time Laura got halfway home. The first few drops of rain were mixed with sleet that quickly turned into small sized hail, with flashes of lightening and booming thunder thrown in for effect. She'd heard of thunder snow, but this was ridiculous!

Laura, who had been speed walking, slowed down and looked around for shelter. The small balls of hail didn't bother her, but the lightening did. She'd reached the part of her walk home that was beautiful on a warm summer day, but now the tall bare trees that ran along both sides of the sidewalk looked to her as nothing more than an invitation for a lightning strike. The nearest refuge was Nancy Blair's sheltered porch. Nancy and her husband Mike had been one of the couples she and Ben had socialized with. Now, both she and Nancy were widows.

Laura reached the porch just as lightning struck, sending one of the trees crashing across the sidewalk. She was still violently shaking from both being wet and the near-death experience when the door opened and Nancy stuck her head out.

"Oh, it's you, Laura! Come in, come in!!"

"Hi, Nancy. Did you hear that big tree go down?" Laura's teeth were chattering.

"Yes, I did. That's what brought me to the door. Seeing you was just a surprise. My goodness, Laura, you're shaking!"

"Oh, I'm so cold!" she shivered. "Nancy, if I had continued walking, that tree would have fallen on me!"

Nancy hugged her. "But it didn't. Come on in and get warmed up. I'll make us some hot chocolate."

"But it would have!" Laura was near tears.

"Life is full of 'what ifs'," Nancy said. "What if your Ben hadn't run the red light? What if my Mike hadn't fallen off the roof of the house?"

Laura took a shaky breath and tried to smile. "You're right, Nancy. Now where's that hot chocolate?"

Nancy handed her a towel. "Follow me to the kitchen and I'll share some juicy news with you."

Laura managed a chuckle "You mean something interesting happened in our small town?"

Nancy's eyes gleamed. "Yes, it did! The most delicious hunk of a man is going to live in the shack at the back of my property. He's out there cleaning the room right now."

"Really? There's a room in that shack?"

Nancy laughed. "I'm surprised you're asking about the room and not the man. The room has always been there, but we've never needed to use it. There's a bed, a dresser, and a space heater so the former owners probably had a worker living there."

"Now you can tell me about the man, but I have a suspicion that I've already seen him."

Nancy raised her eyebrows. "Really?"

Laura nodded. "In fact, Joan's husband literally ran into him. Almost knocked him off his feet. Is he tall, bald, with the beginnings of a black beard?"

"Yes, that's him! His name is Bob Miller. His car broke down and he used all his money buying parts to fix it, so he needs a place to stay, and until his car is repaired, he's going to work here for free!"

Laura's brow raised. "Are you going to do any checking on him? How do you know that he's as good as he looks?"

A concerned look flashed across Nancy's face. "You mean dangerous?"

Laura nodded.

"I guess I didn't think enough about it because I need help so badly. I've worn myself out trying to do all the work by myself."

"Did he say how long it was going to take for his car to be fixed?"

"No, he didn't, but how long can it take for parts to be shipped?"

Laura shrugged. "I'm probably seeing a problem where there isn't one. Forget about what I said. He looked like a good citizen to me, and if you need help that badly, just be glad that you found him."

"Good." After setting two cups of steaming hot chocolate on the table, she turned to Laura. "Now, tell me about our friend Joan."

It was a short storm that ended as quickly as it started. George, aka Bob Miller, was on his way to the main house when he happened to see the tall blond struggling to get around the top of a fallen tree that was spread across the sidewalk.

His hand reached up and wiped the saliva off his chin. Just watching the leggy blond picking her way around the tree was making his mouth water.

# Chapter 39

The clattering of dishes and the tantalizing smell of bacon made its way down into the deep hole where Joan had hidden to escape reality. Afraid to open her eyes, she quietly listened and smelled. Several times she had crawled out of the hole only to rush back in when physical and mental pain slammed into her. In the hole, neither pain nor her attacker could find her.

Her ears picked up the sound of footsteps outside her door. He was coming back! Just the thought of his evil grin showing the chipped front tooth that she'd found so enchanting at first was enough to send her sliding back down into safety.

"Any signs of improvement?" John asked the nurse who had accompanied him to his wife's room.

The nurse studied Joan's chart. "Not really. One visitor did report she had a moment of awareness. But that lasted only a few seconds."

The nurse left the room when John's sobs brought tears to her eyes.

The sound of someone sobbing made its way into Joan's hiding place. George was at it again, but it surprised her that it was a man's sob that she heard. As far as she knew, George only inflicted pain on women. If he were into torturing men, the authorities knew nothing about it. Her first impulse was to reach out and comfort the man, but to do that she'd have to climb out of her safe place.

She dismissed the impulse with a shudder.

# Chapter 40

George experienced a moment of panic when he woke up in a room so dark he couldn't see his hand in front of his face. The moment passed quickly when he remembered where he was. The windowless room in the shed was adequate as long as the weather didn't get too cold. But since he was supposed to be here just long enough for his car to be fixed, there was no reason for that issue to even be discussed. If he played his cards right, by the time the really cold weather arrived he'd be sleeping in the big house, and not alone. Picturing himself in bed with the petite dark-haired owner brought its own problem; his body only responded to tall-leggy blonds. Could he claim a war injury? Maybe a medical problem?

Having to go to the big house to use the bathroom was getting old, especially this morning when his bladder was screaming to be emptied. Breakfast and relief were waiting for him there, but he knew that as soon as he stepped into the house, Nancy would start a conversation before he could get to the bathroom. It was in desperation that he rushed to the back of the shed to relieve himself.

He was in the middle of a satisfied sigh when he noticed movement in the cul-de-sac one street over. Two kids were chasing a dog that had something red in its mouth, and a female voice was yelling, "Roscoe, come back here!" George was zipping up his pants when he noticed that another person had joined the chase. Even from this distance, George recognized the familiar blond who managed to catch the dog and pry something out of its mouth. While pointing an accusing finger at the two kids, she held up the remains of a chewed-up hat with most of the wide brim missing.

It was good to know that the blond was a close neighbor.

He was wondering what chores Nancy would assign him today as he hurried to the big house where the wonderful smell of coffee and bacon beckoned him. Yesterday he had cleaned cabins after the vacationers had moved out, and then he had laundered their bedding and towels.

"Good morning, Bob," Nancy greeted him when he entered the dining room. The empty, dirty plates in front of the two couples, who were already at the table, indicated that they had finished their breakfast.

"Morning everyone," George replied. "Sure smells good in here!"

Nancy chided him, "You're late, Bob, but there's still some food left. I'll pour you a cup of coffee while you fill your plate. Everything is on the stove in the kitchen."

George looked chagrinned. "I'm sorry I'm late, but since the shed doesn't have a window, it's hard for me to judge the time in the morning."

"No watch?" Nancy asked.

He shook his head.

"No iPhone?"

Again, he shook his head.

"I know there's a clock and a watch around here somewhere," Nancy commented. "When I find them, I'll give them to you. And you know what else I'm going to give you?"

George raised his eyebrows.

Nancy left the room and came back with several candles, a candleholder, and a book of matches. "'It's better to light a candle than to curse the darkness,'" she quoted as she handed them to George.

"Why, thank you! This is all much appreciated!" he replied. "What do you have me scheduled to do today?"

"How are you at chopping down trees?" she asked.

He chuckled. "Can't say that I've ever done it, but I'm not saying that I can't do it. How big is the tree?"

"Not too big. It's just that it's rotted and if it falls on its own, it's going to land on the deck. Now go fill your plate so that I can clean up the kitchen."

Nancy smiled as she watched her handsome handyman disappear into the kitchen. The arrangement was working so well, she hoped it was going to take a long time for Bob's car to be fixed.

George smiled to himself as he went into the kitchen to load his plate with pancakes, eggs, and bacon. The arrangement was working so well, he wondered how long he could play the part of a handyman before Nancy started to ask questions about his car.

# Chapter 41

"….and then the two of us hid behind a big tree and watched Mr. Luce yell threats about what he was going to do when he caught us. You were so scared, you peed your pants. Do you remember that, Joan?"

Laura leaned back and studied Joan's face, hoping to see some glimmer of life. Every morning for the past month she'd visited Joan at the Rehab Center and just talked to her. The only reaction she'd ever gotten was the time she mentioned the stranger she'd seen in town. Physically, Joan was healing. The named carved into her forehead had scabbed over, and although her fingers were still bandaged, she didn't flinch from the simplest touch. But mentally, Joan had shut out the world and nothing Laura or Dr. Zumwalt tried had reached into her safe zone.

Joan, who had always taken pride in her appearance, seemed to have no concern over her unbrushed hair. Laura pulled out a brush of her own, hoping to soothe her friend with it. "Joan, remember how we used to play with each other's hair? We did up-sweeps, braids, ponytails, French twists…remember?"

She didn't even blink.

After a few strokes, she felt Joan's body relax, and a sigh of pleasure made it past her closed lips. It didn't take many more strokes before steady breathing told Laura that Joan had fallen asleep. After tucking the covers around her, Laura quietly slipped out of the room.

George Knox, dressed in his work clothes, quickly stepped into a waiting room to avoid being seen by the familiar blond who paused before leaving a room to softly exclaim, "Sleep well, Joan."

Whew! That was close, but mission accomplished; he'd found Joan. If the blond had seen him, it wasn't that he'd be recognized for who he truly was, it just would have been awkward trying to explain why Nancy's handyman was in the Rehab Center.

Not finishing the Joan project was eating at him. It was all because that damn towel had caught fire, and it didn't help that he couldn't get Joan's friend out of his mind. She was tempting him to break the rule that a project, once started, had to be finished before starting a new one. He was a stickler for rules, but didn't someone once say that all rules were made to be broken?

A glance at Nancy's dead husband's watch told him that it was time to head back to the bed and breakfast. Since Nancy was gone for the day, he had "borrowed" the company's van for the drive into town to check out Joan's location. The last thing he wanted to do was screw up his perfect living situation, and taking the van without Nancy's permission could do that. Then he remembered the one chore he still had to do before her return. The remains of a healthy bowel movement that had caused the toilet in cabin three to overflow needed to be cleaned. He gagged just thinking about it.

Maybe this job wasn't so wonderful after all.

# Chapter 42

Laura walked out of A Touch of Color with a smile on her face and a check in her hand. Commissioned painting jobs that Elizabeth had sent her way had kept her busy for weeks. The arrival of the insurance check had made life a lot brighter now that she didn't have to worry about losing the house.

A quick visit to Joan, and then she planned on going to the grocery store to pick up ingredients for tonight's dinner. The numerous painting jobs had taken up time that she should have been spending with her kids, at least feeding them something other than delivered pizzas. It was a guilty conscience that was sending her to the store to buy chicken, noodles, and potatoes to make their favorite meal.

Laura entered the Rehab Center and found Joan strapped in a wheelchair facing a large picture window. Joan's dead eyes didn't register the sweeping view of a large landscaped area that included an ice-covered pond and a frozen waterfall.

"Any sign of improvement?" she asked a worker who was passing by. The woman just shook her head and kept walking.

Laura did what she had been doing for weeks. She pulled up a chair, sat down, and started talking.

"Hi, Joan, it's me! What shall we talk about today? How about the time we stuffed the ballot box and got the linebacker of our football team elected Homecoming Queen?"

No reaction.

"How about this. Do you recall your big crush on the new boy from France who transferred into our eighth-grade class? To get his attention, you tried to learn to speak French by studying a textbook. The only thing the textbook didn't tell you was how to pronounce the words."

Laura studied Joan's face.

"You don't remember how hard he laughed when you spoke to him in French?"

Joan didn't even blink.

Laura sat for a while, wondering if she could ever come up with a memory that would get a reaction from her friend. Their history went way back to early childhood. Their lives had been so intertwined that as they matured, even their monthly periods had lined up together.

Laura jumped out of her chair so fast it toppled over in her rush to the front desk.

"May I help you?" asked the receptionist.

"I need to speak to Joan's doctor. It's important."

The receptionist looked at Laura with skeptical eyes.

"You want to complain about something? You have to know that the staff is excellent here, and your friend Joan is getting the best care possible."

Laura shook her head. "It's not a complaint, believe me. I just need to ask her doctor a question."

The receptionist picked up the phone and pushed a button. "A friend of Joan's is here claiming she has an important question to ask you."

Laura couldn't hear what the doctor said, but evidentially the request was granted.

"Dr. Susan Daily will see you now. Go down the hall to the second door on your right. She's waiting for you."

Dr. Daily, a very pretty dark-haired woman with dimples in both cheeks, was sitting behind her desk smiling when Laura entered the room.

"Hello, Dr. Daily. My name is Laura Baker, and I'm a lifelong friend of one of your patients, Joan."

"I'm glad to meet one of Joan's friends. I notice that you visit her every day."

"Yes, I do. We have so many memories that I keep hoping that one of these days I'll mention one that she will react to. So far, I haven't been very successful."

"The receptionist said that you had a question?"

"While talking to her today, I remembered that we were so close that when we matured, our periods lined up together. Since I just finished mine, it made me wonder about Joan. She's been in here long enough to have had one, or possibly two periods. My question is, did she?"

Dr. Daily thought for a minute. "I don't believe she did, but I will check her records to see if one of the workers mentioned it."

Laura chewed her lower lip. How far should she push the question? "Dr. Daily, the man who is responsible for her present condition probably had sex with her, too. There is a chance that Joan could be pregnant."

Dr. Daily sighed. "I sincerely hope not. In Joan's condition, I'm not sure she can handle a pregnancy."

"You don't understand. Joan has been trying for years to get pregnant. She and her husband have spent a small fortune trying to achieve that. This might be the one subject that would get a rise out of her."

"If she really wants a baby that badly, there is that possibility, but traumatic events often disrupts the menstrual cycle. However, in this case I will order the test immediately."

Laura left the Rehab Center with mixed emotions. After all the men Joan had sex with trying to get pregnant, wouldn't it be ironic if the one who made it happen was a serial killer?

She was so preoccupied that she failed to stop at the grocery store on her way home. All her good intentions flew out the window and to the delight of Beth and Teddy, yet another pizza was delivered to their door.

# Chapter 43

For the past three days, Laura, had been hanging around her mailbox hoping that this was the day the mail carrier would bring her pre-ordered copy of Josh Lang's new book. It had hit the market last week and today Josh was signing books between noon and two o'clock at Horizon's, the only bookstore in town. What was the point of pre-ordering if you didn't get your book before it was available to the general public?

Ah, she could hear a vehicle stopping and starting, the sound of the mail being delivered to her neighbors. Today had to be the day.

When the truck pulled up to her mailbox, Tom stuck his arm out the window and handed Laura a package. "Good morning, Mrs. Baker! You're looking mighty pretty today."

Laura dipped her head and made a mini-bow. "Why, thank you, Tom. I might say the same about you. Your baby must be sleeping through the night because the bags under your eyes are much smaller than the last time I saw you."

He threw back his head and laughed. "No, he's still not sleeping through the night. I just have gotten more creative with earplugs and pillows."

"Oh, your poor wife!" Laura scolded.

"Hey, I work and she doesn't!"

"Get out of here, Tom," Laura chuckled. "Finish your route and go home and relieve your wife. What she does all day is hard work, too."

Tom put the truck in gear and headed for the next mailbox. "Enjoy your book," he called out the window.

Laura glanced at her watch and realized that it was later than she thought. Unless she wanted to be at the end of a long line of women waiting to get their books signed, she had less than an hour to get ready.

After a quick shower, shampoo, and hastily applied makeup, she was ready to grab her old coat when her eyes fell upon the beautiful coat that she'd found in the resale store. For some reason, she wanted to

111

look especially nice for her first encounter with Josh since the near-drowning incident. Would he even remember her? After all, his wife had just died and his thoughts had to have been elsewhere.

With one last glance in the mirror, she picked up the book and was heading for the door when the phone rang.

"Hello?"

"Mrs. Baker?"

"Yes."

"It's Jane," the woman on the other line said. When Laura didn't answer right away she continued, "I'm the receptionist at Joan's Rehab Center."

"I know who you are. What's up?"

"Dr. Susan Daily asked me to call you. She would like you to meet with her."

"Oh, sure. I visit Joan every day and I plan on being there this afternoon. I can meet with her then."

"Uh, later is not what Dr. Daily has in mind. She'd like you here as soon as possible."

Laura glanced down at the book she was holding.

"Really? What's so important that it can't wait until later this afternoon?"

There was silence on the other end of the phone.

Laura sighed. "Okay, if that's what she wants, it must be important. Tell her I'm on my way."


Thirty minutes later Laura was seated in Dr. Daily's office staring at a lab report. Joan was pregnant. That a serial killer's sperm had accomplished what a fertility clinic, along with Ben, and who knows how many other eager participants, couldn't was just plain cruel. Too shocked to say anything, she sat and stared at the report.

The silence in the room was shattered when the door flew open and John rushed in. "Did something happen? Is she okay? Has there been a breakthrough?"

"Good morning, John. Joan's condition hasn't changed but there is a situation that we have to talk about. Have a seat."

"Oh, hi, Laura. I didn't know you'd be here, too."

Dr. Daily answered before Laura could say a word. "I wanted both of you here for several reasons. John, Laura knows your wife better than you do."

John didn't look surprised. "I know that. So, what's going on?"

Dr. Daily looked at Laura. "Hand him the report, please."

It took just one word on the report to have John on his feet yelling. "Pregnant? That evil son-of-a-bitch got my wife pregnant?"

Dr. Daily motioned to his chair. "Sit down and let's talk about this quietly, please. Maybe you can tell us why you immediately thought George Knox was the father. Could it be you?"

John's face turned red. "Uh, I don't think so. True, I was home that whole week, but we never had sex. She tried, kept saying it was her fertile period, but I was tired from all the traveling I do for my job. All I wanted to do was sleep...but not with her."

Neither woman commented on his statement.

John continued. "So, let's schedule the abortion. There's no way on earth I'm raising the kid of that crazed serial killer."

Laura raised her eyebrows. "Don't you think Joan has a say in this decision?"

John shrugged. "What's the point of even asking her? I know you talk to her every day, and so do I. Nothing we've said has gotten any kind of reaction from her. What makes you think this would be any different?"

Dr. Daily said, "Dr. Zumwalt is on his way. Let's wait for him to get here before we discuss this any further."

"I really don't care what the good doctor has to say," John fumed. "I insist on an abortion. He's not the one who would be saddled with raising something that sick son-of-a-bitch fathered!"

"B...b...but," Laura stammered. "I think that the least we can do is try. John, I don't think you know the lengths Joan went to trying to get pregnant."

"What do you mean I don't know? Of course I know! I'm her husband, for heaven's sake!"

Laura rolled her eyes.

John searched her face with narrowed eyes. "What? What's with the eye rolling, Laura? You know something I don't?"

Before she could answer, the door opened and Dr. Zumwalt stepped into the room. "Sorry to be late. I had a session that ran a bit overtime. What have I missed?"

"Have a seat, Dr. Zumwalt," Dr. Daily welcomed him. "I'm just glad you could make it on such short notice. It seems we have a bit of a problem here. John, please hand the lab report to the doctor."

Dr. Zumwalt's face didn't reveal what he was feeling; the others didn't say a word, just waited. Finally, he cleared his throat. "You are right. This is a problem."

John got to his feet, towering over the seated doctor. "No, it's not a problem, Dr. Zumwalt. I demand an abortion immediately!"

The psychiatrist looked up at him. "Whoa, let's think about this before we do anything rash."

"Yeah, you just have fun thinking about it," John yelled, waving his fingers in the doctor's face. "I'm the one who is going to be stuck raising that evil man's spawn, and I'm telling you now, I'm not going to do it!"

Laura watched the two sparring men and remembered the tears Joan had shed each month when menstrual blood stained her underpants shouting the message that she'd failed again. Joan had told her that John had gone along with the very expensive but failed experiments at the fertility clinic only because she insisted. She also said that he was happy with their childless marriage but because he loved her, he had been very supportive even though the costly procedures had depleted their savings. Would he be surprised to know how far his wife had gone in search of a sperm donor? And that one of them had been his friend, Ben? How many more unknown donors were there? Only she and Dr. Zumwalt knew the extent of Joan's obsession. John would never see the picture that was burned into her memory of Joan waving to her from the floral truck as she drove off with the killer. Undoubtedly, she had seen the handsome but deadly George Knox as the next donor.

"....and that's final!" John yelled and the door slammed shut behind him.

Laura blinked. What had she missed?

Dr. Daily, who had sat quietly through the encounter, finally spoke. "That's it, then. Legally, he has the right to make decisions because Joan is incompetent right now. The problem is that Joan has some healing to do before we can schedule anything. That monster did some serious internal damage to her."

Laura jumped to her feet. "Oh my God! That's…that's…." Collapsing back onto the chair, she covered her face with her hands, and sobbed. "My poor Joan! Does John know the extent of her damage?"

The doctor sighed. "No, he doesn't. I felt that the man had been battered enough emotionally as it was. And yes, I will tell him."

"But we can tell her that she's pregnant, can't we?" Laura pleaded. "For weeks now I've been talking to her every day, trying to find a subject that would get a rise out of her. Don't you think telling her that she's pregnant might be the shock that jars her out of her comatose state?"

Dr. Zumwalt agreed. "Yes, it could, but it also could drive her further into that state. How is she going to feel about carrying a child who was fathered by the man who tortured her with the intent to murder her?"

Laura voice was firm when she spoke. "Dr. Zumwalt, you and I know that Joan's obsession to be a mother was driving her to do dangerous things. She needs to be told even if the knowledge could send her deeper into herself."

Dr. Daily was listening, wondering what dangerous things Joan had done trying to get pregnant. "I need to talk to our legal department before we do anything. Let's adjourn, and I'll get back to both of you when I know how much we can do without first obtaining her husband's permission. Consider this meeting adjourned."

Feeling both sad and frustrated with how the meeting had gone, Laura walked out of Dr. Daily's office and headed for Joan's room. As she got closer, she could hear the sound of a man sobbing. It was John.

Not wanting to intrude on John's grieving time with his wife, she walked past Joan's door and headed for the exit. It might be a selfish thing to even consider doing such a frivolous thing as getting an author's autograph when her best friend was in such a terrible situation, but John was with her, and what was going to happen to Joan was now in his hands.

If she hurried, Josh Lang might still be autographing books.

# Chapter 44

Finding a parking place near Horizon's Book Store always was a problem; today it was impossible. A new parking garage had recently been added to ease the town's problem, but it was three blocks away. Laura kept driving around, hoping a parking spot would open even though Josh's signing hours were over and he probably was no longer at the store. Finally, a car that was parked right in front of Horizon's pulled out of its spot and drove away, Laura wasted no time and zipped into the spot. Parallel parking was never her favorite thing to do, but she got the job done, albeit a bit crooked.

Josh was scribbling his name in the last fan's book, discussing the plot of his last novel when he looked up and let the conversation die.

Perfume. Josh smelled Marie's perfume. From the store's window, he could see a woman crawling out of a car. Time stopped. From the back, she looked just like Marie. Same body shape, same manner of movements, and that coat! How many times had held it while she slipped her arms in, and how many times had he kissed the back of her neck while helping her? Was he hallucinating? When the woman turned around, he let out a breath that he hadn't been aware that he was holding. He couldn't remember where, but somewhere he had seen that face. It was a pretty face, but it wasn't Marie's.

As the woman headed for the entrance of the bookstore the odor intensified. Josh mumbled something to the puzzled lady and raced out the store's back door.

Laura dashed into the store hoping she hadn't missed the opportunity to have her book signed. Horizon always had a table near the front entrance where the author sat while signing his book. She had no trouble finding the table, but the only person there was a woman who was holding one of Josh's books.

"I missed him, didn't I?" Laura panted.

Before she answered, the woman took a good look at the very attractive tall blond who had caused the author to flee the building. "Yes, you did. Does he know you?"

Laura raised her eyebrows. "Why do you ask?"

"We were having a lovely conversation until he looked out the window and saw you."

"So, where is he?"

The woman shrugged. "I have no idea, but he literally ran out the back door. At that speed, he could be in the next county by now. And we were having such a nice conversation."

"I'm sorry I chased him away, but I have no idea why I would. I did meet him once, but his wife had just died and he was very upset. I doubt that he remembers me."

"Oh, he remembers you all right! You should have seen his face!"

"Really? I find that hard to believe."

"Well, believe it!" She pointed to the book Laura was holding. "Don't waste your time waiting for him to come back to sign your book. Josh Lang is long gone."

Laura stammered, "I...I...I really don't understand why he felt the need to run away."

"Well," the lady said as she turned to leave. "Whatever you did, he's terrified of you."


Josh leaned up against the hood of his car, closed his eyes and tried to calm his racing heart. Happenings like this couldn't be explained so therefore they weren't rational. But damn it, the lady had been wearing one of Marie's coats. He'd swear to that, plus she did resemble her a little.

But what was that perfume bit all about? The first time that happened was when he rescued the woman at the lake. His eyes flew open. That's why the woman's face looked familiar! He had been in such a rush to head downstate to arrange Marie's funeral he hadn't paid much attention, but he was sure she was the same lady who was humming their song when he rescued her.

His fist came down hard on the car's hood. This craziness had to stop!

# Chapter 45

George was finding it easy to assume the character of Bob Miller. After all, he'd played the role for most of the ten years he was in prison. Sometimes when Bob's cloying niceness made him nauseated, he either retreated to his shack and quietly mouthed profanity, or he grabbed an ax and vigorously chopped wood.

Several times he had made the trip to the Rehab Center hoping to find the entrance to Joan's room unguarded. So far, that hadn't happened, but the longer the unsuccessful search for him went on, the sooner things would relax. When that occurred, he'd be there to finish off the Joan project and then he would start a new one.

He'd found that the leggy blond who lived a street away was called Laura. Some evenings she and her two kids played ball in the cul-de-sac along with a dog named Roscoe. His supply of torture instruments was growing. It was just a matter of time, and in his secure living arrangement, he had a lot of it.

The media referred to him as the Gentleman Serial Killer. Tall, handsome, dimples in both cheeks and a full head of black hair, he'd cause quite a stir when he moved into a town, and under an assumed name he would work his way into the life of the community. Such a handsome bachelor had no problem attracting female companions, and soon he would be seen around town escorting a tall blond woman who had no idea that she was to become his next victim. To make torturing her more enjoyable, he would court her like a Puritanical gentleman until he was sure she was in love with him.

And then she would disappear.

He'd join the community in the search for her, attend prayer circles, and even shed tears with her family. By moving to different states and communities, for years he had managed to get away with his evil deeds until one of his half-dead victims escaped and staggered into town with the name Knox tattooed on her forehead. The people had no idea who Knox was, but when the woman pointed a bloody finger at a pillar of the community, there were gasps of disbelief.

The discovery of a dozen similar unsolved cases across the country sent George to prison for life with no hope of parole.

That sentence was negated by Larry's failure to observe safety rules.


Today, his shaved head, his neatly trimmed black beard, and brown contacts covering his blue eyes, gave him a completely different look than the one he had when he was called the Gentleman Serial Killer. No one questioned him as he walked the halls of the Rehab Center. He had discovered early in life that if you act as if you know what you're doing, no one asks questions, but in case someone did, he had a story to cover his presence. Quite handsome in Mike's casual clothes, he got smiles from a few workers and a nod from several therapists.

As he got closer to Joan's room, he was pleased to see that instead of two guards outside her door, today there was just one. Not wanting the guard to see him, he went through the motions of looking at his watch and then acting distressed as if he were late for something. His abrupt change of direction was a surprise to the two people who were right behind him.

"Oh, I'm so sorry!" George exclaimed.

Laura was saved from falling by the man walking with her. "Oh, thank you, Reverend Shaffer!"

George watched the reverend grin suggestively at her. "Believe me, it was my pleasure!"

George bristled. How dare the man touch her? She was his property! Trying hard to hide his instant fury, he managed to sound quite rational when he again said, "I am so sorry!"

Laura smiled. "No harm done."

George looked at the Reverend, and seeing an opportunity, asked, "Are you the minister of a church here in town? I'm new, and I've been looking for one."

The reverend's face brightened. "Why, yes I am! It's the West Side Community Church on M-72 west of town."

"Good to know! I just might drop in one of these Sundays."

"This man delivers remarkable sermons," Laura added, offering George her hand. "That's my church, and I promise you won't be disappointed. By the way, I'm Laura Baker. We've never formally met, but I have seen you around town, and I understand that you are working for my friend, Nancy."

George's mind raced as he shook her hand. What was his name? Bob. Yes, that was it. "Glad to meet the two of you! My name is Bob Miller, and yes, I'm temporarily working at the bed and breakfast while my car is being repaired."

"Well, Nancy is quite pleased with the arrangement. I'm sure she's wishing that it will take a lot of time to fix your car."

George lowered his eyes as if embarrassed. "That's nice of you to say that."

The reverend shook his hand. "Glad to meet you, Bob. Are you here to visit someone?"

George's mind flashed back to his prison days. "No one in particular. I just look for someone who appears to be lonely and in need of a friend to pray with. I feel so blessed that I'm able to help someone who is longing to get in touch with our Lord and Savior."

"Praise the Lord!" Rev. Shaffer exclaimed. "Bob, the world needs more people like you. May I ask if you've had the opportunity to pray with Ida Fox?"

George looked puzzled. "Can't rightly say that I have. Why do you ask?"

"She's also a member of my congregation. Next time you're here, I'd appreciate it if you would stop in and pray with her. She's a widow, and since her children live on the other side of the country, she doesn't get very many visitors."

"What's her problem?"

"Her legs are paralyzed. She took a brutal fall last winter and got banged up pretty bad. The Center feels with enough therapy and encouragement, someday she'll walk."

"Considerate it done," George replied, noticing that Laura was looking quite interested.

"Good! She's in the room right next to the office."

"I'll check in with her on the way out. And you can expect to see me next Sunday."

122

"Good! I'm so glad we literally bumped into each other today!" the reverend chuckled.

George grinned. "Hey, so am I."

Laura tugged on the preacher's sleeve. "We best get going. Joan has therapy in half an hour."

George glanced at his watch. Unless he wanted to add being late to the list of questions Nancy would be asking when he got back, he needed to hurry.

In his rush, he almost forgot to find Ida's room. Since it was looking like the church was the way to get close to Laura, anything he could do to ingratiate himself to the minister couldn't be passed up.

Through her partially opened door, he could see what could have been an attractive older woman if her face hadn't been contorted by fear. A sheen of perspiration covered her forehead as she stood by her bed, her legs shaking with the effort to remain standing. Her sigh of failure was followed by her collapse back onto the bed. After a few deep breaths, she stood up and repeated the exercise. Remembering all the bogus healing services he had conducted while in prison, an idea occurred to him. Since there was nothing holding Ida back but the fear of falling, he could just picture how impressive his next healing service was going to be. Ida was going to rise up out of the much-hated wheelchair and walk.

George left the Rehab Center feeling quite pleased with himself.

# Chapter 46

A week had passed since he'd last been at the Rehab Center. The list of jobs that had been neglected since Nancy's husband died a year ago was still long even after George's long days of working on the projects.

He stepped out of the shack in time to see Nancy waving goodbye to departing guests. His plan of slipping into town to buy replacement parts for a vacuum cleaner while dressed in one of Mike's dressier outfits hadn't worked. She wouldn't like it because she counted it as free advertising when he paraded in town with the name of her business embroiled on his jacket.

What she would never know was that after he bought the parts, he was going to go to the Rehab Center to check on Joan. Looking professional raised fewer questions about his presence at the Center than when he wore his work uniform. Eventually they were going to get lax on guarding her room and he wanted to be there when they did. If ever his presence was questioned, he could always fall back on his story about praying with the patients.

Nancy glanced over to watch Bob walk to the truck. Goodness, how handsome he looked in Mike's clothes! But why was he so dressed-up when he was just going to town to buy replacement parts for a vacuum cleaner?

She was surprised at her sudden feeling of possessiveness. Was he dressed to impress some woman in town? He was hers, and she didn't want to share him! The sudden stab of jealousy surprised her along with the thought that maybe she didn't have the right to be jealous. It was only reasonable to think that a man as handsome, witty, and kind as Bob had a family somewhere. Every time she tried to get him to talk about himself, he managed to turn the subject of the conversation back to her. By now, he knew more about her than her own mother did.

Another thing puzzled her. He was here because his car was being repaired, but the subject never came up. She knew she could inquire about it, but she was afraid to ask because she really didn't want to hear that it was repaired and he was leaving. Just thinking about that happening took the air out of her lungs, leaving her with a revelation; she had deep feelings for the man. The truth hit her with such force she leaned against a tree for support.

# Chapter 47

Laura walked out of Dr. Daily's office fighting the urge to slam the door. She was tired of excuses.

"Mrs. Baker, you know we can't rush these things!"

"Mrs. Baker, the head of our legal counsel is on vacation."

"Mrs. Baker, we have to follow the rules."

"Mrs. Baker, it won't be much longer. We have to be patient about these things."

"Mrs. Baker, I told you I'd let you know if I've heard anything."

"Mrs. Baker? Oh, it's you again. No, nothing to report."

Muttering to herself, she walked toward Joan's room with her head down and almost missed seeing Nancy's handyman approaching the room. Today he had on an outfit that she was sure she had seen Mike wearing. In fact, Ben had commented on how much he liked it.

That's when she noticed that the chair outside the room was vacant. Where was the guard? With no one to stop him, Laura saw Bob entering Joan's room.

"Bob, would you please wait?" she called out to him.

*So close!* George closed his eyes and swore under his breath. Putting a pious look on his face, he turned and saw that it was his Laura who had stopped him. He liked to think of her as *his* Laura because it really was just a matter of time.

"Well, hello there, Miss Laura! How nice to run into you again!" he purred.

"Bob, no one is supposed to go into Joan's room without permission from the guard."

George looked puzzled. "Guard? I don't see a guard. And why would she need a guard? Is she some kind of dangerous criminal?"

"Well, a guard should be here and I can't imagine why he's not. She was attacked by a serial killer. The police can't find him, so he's still out there. It's been on the news."

"Oh, my! How awful! Is your friend going to be all right?"

126

"Only time will tell, but why were you going into her room? Do you know her?"

"No, I don't know her. I was just going to ask her if she wanted someone to pray with her. Remember, I told you and the reverend yesterday that this is what I do? Patients find it to be an uplifting experience."

"It probably is, but since Joan is incapable of communicating, I think you should leave. Oh, I hear someone coming."

From down the hall, they could hear the sound of pounding feet getting closer. Finally, a panting man skidded to a stop in front of them and flopped down on the empty chair.

"Whoa," he exclaimed. "That was close!"

"Where were you?" Laura demanded.

The guard's face turned red. "Uh, I had an emergency, if you know what I mean?" His eyebrows danced like black caterpillars.

"But Joan's door was wide open. Anyone, including the serial killer, could have walked right in! In fact, Bob did."

The guard looked at George and smiled. "This guy, a serial killer? I think not!"

George smiled. "So, you are an expert on what a serial killer looks like?"

"I should hope so. I've been in law enforcement all my adult life, and you, sir, are not a serial killer."

George laughed. "I'll sleep better tonight knowing that. Well, God's work is done for today, so I'm going to head back to Nancy's place."

Laura waved to him as he turned to leave. "Tell her I said, 'Hi' and that I'll call her tomorrow."

What an extraordinary man! That he was extremely handsome was just icing on an already delicious cake. Kind, considerate, and obviously religious, he was one of a kind. There was a huge smile on her face when she entered Joan's room, only to find her friend sound asleep.

Perhaps it was best that she was asleep because, tired of excuses, Laura had decided that today was the day that she was going to tell her about her pregnancy. So far, the only reaction she had gotten from Joan was during their first conversation when she'd mentioned seeing a stranger in town. Anyhow, since Joan wasn't talking, no one would ever know that she'd been told that she was pregnant before the lawyers had come back with a decision.

Laura stood for a moment and quietly studied her best friend. Her forehead was scabbed but the name was still readable. What kind of devil lived inside the heart of George Knox? And where was he? Closing her eyes, she was silently praying for her childhood friend when a thought entered her mind. Having someone to pray with would be wonderful.

Someone like Bob.


Dressed in his uniform, George walked out of his shack with the repair parts in his hand and wild thoughts in his head. Fixing the vacuum should be easy enough even if his mind was elsewhere. Now that there was just one guard at Joan's door, it should be easy enough to create a situation that would get rid of him for a few minutes. That's all the time he would need to finish the Joan project.

But there was no hurry. Miss Laura had yet to be wooed, dined, and romanced by The Gentleman Serial Killer.

# Chapter 48

Rev. Jacob Shaffer stood behind the pulpit and beamed at the crowd that was streaming into his West Side Community Church. Among the sea of faces he spotted Laura Baker who was looking very attractive today in her Sunday-go-to-meetin' clothes. He smiled to himself as he remembered his mother's voice saying that phrase every Sunday as she dragged him and his brother kicking and screaming out of bed. Did people today have special church outfits? His doubt was justified by noticing that many in the audience were wearing jeans. Dressing for church in your Sunday-go-to-meetin' clothes was a thing of the past.

The door that connected the education building to the church flew open and a laughing Bob Miller led a noisy group of people into the sanctuary. The reverend watched Bob's Bible study class quieting down when they realized there was already a full auditorium waiting for the 11:00 service to begin.

"I don't see any empty seats," he heard Bob stage-whispering to the group. "Let's head for the balcony."

How had Bob done it? In just a few weeks, his Bible study group had more than doubled itself. Right now, they were following Bob as if he were some sort of a rock star. An atmosphere of excitement even extended to the choir members who were singing the opening song with energy and gusto.

After the song was finished, he stepped to the pulpit and uttered, "Let us pray."

Waiting for the shuffle of feet and a cough here and there to settle down, he spent the moments formulating the words and sentences that he would include in his prayer. Who he really wanted to thank was Bob Miller for livening up and enlarging his congregation, but that would come later.

With exception of one, all heads were bowed. George took the opportunity from his high seat in the balcony to scan the crowd below him. There she was. Somehow, he had to manage running into her before she made it out the door after the service.

The last rich organ notes of the closing song were still vibrating in the air when George slipped out of his seat and headed for the main entrance. His plan was to wait for Laura to emerge and then accidentally bump into her after she'd shaken hands with the minister. Because many wanted to stop and chat with Rev. Shaffer, the line was moving slowly, agitating the ever-churning blackness inside him.


Laura left the church and headed in the direction of her car. It was times like this that losing Ben hit the hardest. After picking up the kids from their junior church in the education building, the four of them would go out for lunch. Remembering those times, she had to admit that not all of them were pleasant. Ben only attended church because she insisted, and by lunchtime, he was straining at the bit for it to end. The last thing he wanted to do was miss his tee time.

Today she felt very much alone with not even her children for company. Helen, another member of her church with children around the same ages as Teddy and Beth, had taken them for a play date. Determined to enjoy the nice day, even though she was alone, she turned her face toward the sun. She was enjoying the warmth of it when her forward momentum was abruptly stopped by a man's hard chest. Looking up, she saw Nancy's handyman grinning down at her.

"I'm so sorry! I wasn't watching where I was going!" she exclaimed.

George congratulated himself on the fancy footwork it had taken to place himself in front of her without looking too obvious.

"Same here!" he laughed. "Are you all right?"

"Just embarrassed," Laura answered.

He stepped back and looked at her. "It's Laura, isn't it?"

"Yes, that's me! And you are Bob. Seems we have a history of bumping into each other."

He looked pleased. "I can see that I made a big impression on you that day at the Rehab Center!"

"Yes, you did," she teased. "It was a big black and blue mark about five inches long and two inches wide."

130

He threw back his head and laughed. Wooing Laura was going to be so much fun!

"Oh, I'm so sorry! I hope today's little accident isn't as impressive. Tell me, Miss Laura, are you heading home right now?"

"Well, yes."

"The reason I asked is that several people from my Bible study group are going out for lunch and we'd be happy to have you join us."

"Really? Where are you going?"

"We have a reservation at the Omelet Shop, the one near the college. Come on, say yes! Good Christian fellowship and a nice lunch. How can you turn that down?"

Laura looked at the handsome man smiling at her and realized that the only thing that wasn't perfect about him was his one chipped front tooth. She thought about walking into her silent house and compared it to having lunch with Bob and his group.

"Sounds too good to pass up! I'll see you there."

He opened his mouth to suggest she leave her car in the church parking lot and ride to the Omelet Shop with him, when he remembered the plan. She was going to be the one to pursue him, not the other way around.

"Good! The reservation is in my name in case you get there first."

Laura was feeling butterflies in her tummy as she walked away from Bob Miller. She hadn't felt butterflies in a long time, and she had to admit, it felt good; there was something about him that excited her. Too bad he didn't offer to give her a ride to the restaurant. Her car would have been perfectly fine in the church parking lot for a few hours.

# Chapter 49

Josh left the chapel where he'd spent the hour meditating while the second service of the day was going on in the church's sanctuary. Sunday morning at the lake was one of their favorite times. Their routine was a cup of coffee on the deck, a leisurely drive to church, and then lunch after the service at the Omelet Shop. He could do the lunch, but he just couldn't face entering the church where he and Marie had spent so many delightful Sunday mornings.

He'd stayed in the chapel and listened for the closing hymn before getting into his car and driving to the restaurant. He knew that when the church door opened, many people would make a mad race to their cars. There was a limited selection of restaurants in the area and on Sunday, tables filled up quickly.

As the hostess welcomed him, he saw that a large area had a reserved sign on it. Not wanting to take up a table for just one person, he agreed when the hostess suggested that he sit at the bar. The seat was facing the entrance and that was fine with him. Since he was eating alone, he could entertain himself by watching the flow of diners.

Before he had time to even read the menu, the door opened and a large group of animated fellow parishioners rushed in and filled the reserved area. He knew there were many social groups within the congregation and he wondered which one this was. It looked as if everyone was having a good time. Maybe he should check it out and if it were something that interested him, he would join. Life in the cabin was all right, but sometimes he felt the need for human interaction.

And then Marie's perfume hit his nose. His head went up, his eyes scanned the group, and his heart skipped a beat. Sitting beside the good-looking guy who obviously was the group's leader, was the woman he'd rescued from the lake. It was with her that he'd first smelled Marie's perfume when it hadn't made any sense. And she did remind him of Marie. The coloring was wrong, but everything else about her was so familiar. It hurt just to watch her.

By the look on her face, she apparently was enamored with the handsome gentleman who was giving her his complete attention. Josh watched in envy. How he missed having an intimate connection with a woman. When he lost Marie, he'd lost so many things that made life rich and worthwhile. He was still watching the couple when the man raised his eyes and searched the bar area. Had he sensed that Josh was staring at him? The man's sweeping gaze stopped when they landed on Josh. For one brief second, the man's brown eyes turned into something terrifying, something not human. Josh wasn't aware that he'd reacted loudly until he became conscious that people were looking at him, including the woman he'd been staring at. When their eyes locked, the smell of Marie's perfume almost choked him.

Laura was basking in the attention of Bob Miller who was treating her like a queen. It had been such a long time since any man had made her every wish his command and she was reveling in it. She was laughing at something he'd said when a startled cry, coming from the bar area, caught her attention. The smile on her face faded when she saw that Josh Lang was staring at her. Their eyes met, froze, and stayed connected until Josh slid off the barstool and rushed out the door, pushing his way through the line of hungry people who were still waiting for a table.

This was the second time Josh had run away from her. And the terrified look on his face! Maybe the woman at the book signing was right; he was scared of her. But why?

Bob nudged her. "Everything all right?"

Laura nodded. "Just saw a lake neighbor. That's all."

Gasping for air, Josh leaned against his car and tried to calm his beating heart. Their song, perfume, and now devil eyes.

# Chapter 50

Laura held Joan's unbandaged hand, careful not to touch the areas where three of her nails had been jerked off and where now there was a hint of the new nails growing in. Her forehead was covered with angry red scars that, unfortunately, still spelled out the name Knox.

Joan's body was mending, but her mind was still as far away as the day they found her. Just watching her friend who had been so vital, so inventive and so mischievous, just lying there brought tears to Laura's eyes. What adventures they'd had together! She missed her old friend.

Was now the time to tell Joan that after years of trying, she was pregnant? What if her reaction to the news sent her further into the hole where she was hiding? The Center's legal council had yet to give an opinion, but just knowing how determined John was about aborting the baby, she already knew what the verdict would be. But none of them knew Joan as well as she did. She deserved to know.

She opened her mouth several times to tell Joan the news, and several times she closed her mouth. Dare she? How much trouble would she be in if Joan's reaction was explosive?

Tough. No matter the consequence, she needed to do this for her friend.

The decision made, she took a deep breath…wait! The sound of many voices coming from outside the room interrupted her train of thought. Something was going on and curiosity sent her running to the door to look out.

Right in the middle of a crowd of doctors, nurses, therapists and every patient who was ambulatory, was Bob Miller. He was standing beside an elderly woman in a wheelchair whose hands were placed together as if she were pleading for something. When Laura walked closer, she saw that the woman in the wheelchair was Ida Fox, the lady whose legs had been paralyzed by the fear of falling.

She watched Bob take a bottle of something out of his pocket, put a drop on his finger, and then anoint Ida Fox's forehead with it.

Then he placed his hand on her head, closed his eyes, and started to pray.

Her breath caught in her throat. Bob was conducting a healing service! His prayer to God to heal Ida was eloquent, spirited, and filled with lines of promising scripture from the Bible. The crowd was murmuring along with the prayer, and when Bob finished, there were several voices that repeated, "Amen."

Silence reigned. And then Ida stirred.

Pushing with her hands on the armrests of her wheelchair, she struggled to stand. With the crowd's encouragement, she put one foot ahead of the other and took a step, and then another step. With tears running down her cheeks, Ida exclaimed, "Thank you, Sweet Jesus! I'm healed!"

George was laughing inside. There was nothing wrong with Ida's legs to begin with. She was just a scared old lady who needed a little magic to overcome her fear. The crowd clapped and cheered, and George hoped he was looking humble while he kept insisting that he was just a vessel who God had chosen to work through.

With a huge smile on his face, George broke away from the crowd when he saw Laura standing some distance away.


When she saw Bob Miller heading her way, all thoughts of staying around to tell Joan the big secret fled in a heartbeat. The closer he got, the more the butterflies in her stomach fluttered around. He was so exciting! She was surprised and disappointed that after the Sunday lunch he hadn't contacted her.

"Bob," she called out. "That was quite a remarkable performance! I'm certainly impressed!"

"Thank you," he replied. "I'm just happy that God can use my meager talents to help such a nice lady like Ida." He lowered his eyes hoping it would make him look humble.

"Are you visiting any more patients this morning?" Laura asked.

"No, I've run out of time," he replied as he turned to leave. "Nancy has a list of things for me to do this afternoon, so I'm going to grab a quick lunch before I go back to work."

Laura held her breath. Was he going to ask her to join him? Her question was answered when he walked past her on his way toward the door. Dare she? Taking a deep breath, she called, "Bob, would you think I was too forward if I invited you to lunch?"

He stopped walking, and when he turned around there was a big smile on his face. "Forward? Of course not! Why, lunch sounds wonderful!"

Laura let out a breath she hadn't been aware she'd been holding. "Should we go back to the Omelet Shop?"

"I like that place," he answered. "How nice of you to invite me."

She hesitated a bit before she added. "Why don't you leave your car here and ride with me to the restaurant?"

"What a great idea!"

George did his best to hide his grin.

# Chapter 51

Laura's lunch companion looked concerned. "Are you all right? Do you need me to pound on your back?"

George had delivered the punch line of a very funny joke just as she'd swallowed a bite of her sandwich.

Unable to speak, she waved a hand and shook her head while she grabbed her water glass and gulped a big swallow. After she recovered, she smiled at him. "I didn't realize that lunch with you was going to be so dangerous! How many more jokes like that do you have?"

"Lots!" he laughed, his brown eyes shining. "But I promise not to tell them to you while you're eating."

Laura was still holding the glass when their eyes met. An electric shock hit her with such force that the glass slipped out of her hand, spilling water over her sandwich and running off the table and onto her lap.

Jumping up, she stepped back. "How clumsy of me!"

"Here, take this," he said, handing her another napkin.

Laura was too embarrassed to talk. What had just happened?

George was wondering the same thing. Whatever it was that occurred when their eyes met was unexpected, strange, and quite pleasant. It was a first for the Gentleman Serial Killer who never got emotionally involved with any of his victims. It would certainly make the job of wooing Laura much more interesting than any of the others.

When the waitress finally appeared to help clean up the spilled water, she asked Laura, "Shall I order you another sandwich?"

Laura paused for a moment before she looked at her companion. "Do you have time? You said you had things to do back at Nancy's."

"I do, but since she's visiting family today and won't be back until dinner time, I'll have time to get everything done before that, so go right ahead and order another one." He chuckled and pointed at her plate. "That is one soggy mess!"

Laura didn't want the lunch to end. Whatever it was that caused her to drop her water glass had to be explored. Would it happen again?

"In that case, I would like another sandwich."

The waitress nodded. "The same kind or another one?"

"The same kind, please."

After the waitress walked away with the ruined sandwich, Laura realized that until her new one arrived, there was going to be a period of time that needed to be filled with conversation. He was half through his own sandwich, so maybe ordering another one wasn't the smart thing to do. What could they talk about? This could be an awkward few minutes.

His voice broke her train of thought. "Tell me," he said, "How is your friend Joan?"

Relieved, the tension went out of her body. He'd picked a topic that she could talk about forever.

George tuned out after a while; stories about their childhood antics held no interest for him. He managed to smile and nod his head at the appropriate time while trying to keep his eyes from crossing.

"…...wasn't that awful? And then, after all the money they'd spent at the fertility clinic with no success, wouldn't you know that the evil man got her pregnant?"

George's eyes flew open, his apathy gone.

"Pregnant?" he croaked. "Joan is pregnant? She can't be!"

His strong reaction to the news puzzled Laura. Why would he care? He didn't even know Joan.

George struggled to get himself under control; he didn't like the way Laura was looking at him.

"I…I was just feeling bad for the poor girl who doesn't need another problem right now. Do you think I should pray with her the next time I'm at the Center?"

Laura nodded in understanding. His strong response about Joan's news was heart-warming. Not only did he feel for her, but he even offered to take time out of his life to visit the Center and pray with her.

The most natural thing for her to do was to reach out and touch his hand. "Bob, it's so sweet that you want to pray with my friend, but

138

she doesn't know she's pregnant, and I don't think she's supposed to be told. She hasn't responded to anything except...."

Her mouth was open to share Joan's reaction when she'd told her about the stranger in town, but just then the waitress arrived at the table with her sandwich.

The conversation never went back to the subject of Joan, and after Laura paid for lunch because she had invited him, she took him back to his car at the Center.

She'd hoped that he would ask to see her again, but he didn't. There was an empty feeling in her heart when she watched him drive away. It was clear that she was the only one who had felt the electric shock when their eyes met.


George was deep in thought as he drove back to the bed and breakfast. For some reason, learning that Joan was pregnant with his child had a sobering effect on him. It made him wonder if any of the others he'd killed were carrying his child when they died. If he hadn't set her house on fire, Joan would have been long dead just like all those who had gone before her and the fact that he had inseminated the victim would have died with her. It would be an interesting and different experience when he finished the Joan project, knowing that by killing her he was also killing his own baby. However, since Laura had said that the husband was pushing for an abortion, it would depend on when the opportunity opened for him to get into her room. And what was that strange sensation that felt like a shock when his eyes had locked with Laura's? He'd never had that happen before with any of the others, so why was it happening with this one? Judging by the surprised look on her face, she had felt it, too.

Distracted by the thoughts that were running through his head, he was unaware that he was drifting into the lane of oncoming traffic. The sudden air horn blast from the logging truck startled him, and his overreaction caused the van to careen to the right and into the ditch. When he finally recovered control, he was looking at a cement bridge abutment inches from the front of his vehicle.

As the dust settled over his van, he laid his head on the steering wheel and shuddered; the last thing he needed was an accident.

He'd told Nancy that he had a driver's license, and then he held his breath waiting for her to ask to see it. Trusting-Nancy didn't, but he knew the police would if he had an accident.

A much-subdued George pulled back into traffic and headed home.

# Chapter 52

"No, Teddy, take that shirt off! You are *not* wearing it again today!"

"But Mom, it's my favorite shirt, and it's only a little dirty."

"Throw it into the laundry basket and put on this one," Laura ordered, handing Teddy another shirt.

"I don't like that one," he pouted.

"And hurry up. The bus will be here in a minute. I don't have time to drive you to school today so you can't miss it. And Beth, don't forget the report we worked on last night. It's by the computer."

Beth came around the corner, her face turned away from her mother.

"Look at me, Beth," Laura ordered, grabbing the girl so that she could see her face. "Lipstick? Where did you get lipstick?"

Beth hung her head. "Your dressing table."

"Young lady, go straight into the bathroom and wash it off! You are *not* going to school looking like that!"

"Ah, Mom. Can't I leave a little bit on?"

"No, you can't! What is this sudden interest in makeup?"

Teddy taunted in a sing-song voice, "Beth has a boyfriend, Beth has a boyfriend!"

"Shut-up, Teddy!" Beth called from the bathroom. "You better shut up or I'm telling Mom how you got into trouble at recess!"

"Really, Teddy? Should I expect a call from Miss Nelson?"

"It was nothing, Mom."

"Nothing? We'll talk about this and Beth's boyfriend when you both get home this afternoon. Now, out the door, you two! I hear the bus!"

The door slammed behind them and Laura collapsed onto a chair. The silence of the house was deafening. Looking around, she saw Beth's forgotten report beside the computer; she had to make a stop at the school on her way to A Spot of Color after all.

Disciplining the children was a new job that had been added to her role as sole-parent. Ben had been the one who had kept them in line, who handed out punishments, and the one who saw that the punishments were actually carried out. She, on the other hand, had the easy job of sympathizing with them while being careful not to undermine Ben's actions. Keeping them in line was a hard job, and she felt that she wasn't doing as well as Ben. The children weren't comfortable with the fact that their understanding and soothing mother had turned into the disciplinarian. Every chance they had, they tested her. Some nights she was so exhausted and all she could think about were the hours of sleep she would get, and stress about how little it was. Those were the nights when either Beth or Teddy, and sometimes both, refused to go to sleep at all. Glasses of milk, glasses of water, a snack, bathroom trips, a bad dream, a fight over what pair of pajamas to wear, arguments over what book she was going to read to them…it went on and on until she yelled at them. These scenes never had a happy ending and the sound of sobbing children made her feel so guilty that sleep came slowly, if it came at all.

Only after all the signs of breakfast were cleared away and the kitchen was once again in pristine condition did Laura allow herself to think about the day ahead. Ben might be gone, but his rigid insistence on her keeping the house clean and tidy had outlived him. One of these days, she assured herself, she was going to walk away from a dirty kitchen just to prove that she could. Just not today.

An hour later, dressed in a linen blue suit with matching shoes, she left the house, ready to face the world as the sole provider for her little family. So far, A Touch of Color had made the job easy, but what if that source dried up? Shouldn't she be looking for additional outlets to market her art?

A quick stop at Beth's school to leave the report in the office with the secretary who promised to deliver it to Beth, and then on to A Touch of Color.

The small parking lot was almost full except for one empty space beside the van from Nancy's bed and breakfast. Laura's eyes widened. Did that mean Bob Miller was in the area? Just the thought of running into him was making her cheeks flush. There would be no reason for a handyman to shop at an art store, but if his truck were here, he had to be somewhere close.

With her new painting tucked under her arm, Laura walked slowly toward the store. Her eyes scanned the parking lot, the sidewalks, and everywhere in-between for a glimpse of him. If he was there, how should she greet him? She had initiated the luncheon date, but he certainly seemed to enjoy her company. Her disappointment when he didn't ask to see her again was still fresh. If she did run into him, how should she act besides surprised?

As she opened the door to A Touch of Color she came face-to-face with Nancy who was just leaving.

"Laura!" Nancy exclaimed. "Just the person I want to see!"

"Well, good morning to you, too!" a surprised and disappointed Laura responded. Bob wasn't in town after all. Trying to hide the empty feeling that swept over her, she forced a smile of welcome to Nancy. "What can I do for you?"

Nancy pointed to the canvas Laura had under her arm. "Elizabeth said you'd be coming in today with a new painting, but I couldn't wait any longer for you to show up. Let me see it!"

"What's the big hurry?" Laura asked.

"I don't want to miss the guy delivering food from The Hatch."

Laura looked at her friend who seemed to be overly excited. "And where would the most exclusive restaurant in town be delivering food?"

"To my house! Oh, I'm so nervous!" Nancy exclaimed. "A reporter and a photographer from the morning paper are interviewing me for an article about my business."

"That is exciting," Laura agreed. "But why are you feeding them?"

"Because I don't want them to write a bad article just because they're hungry!"

Laura laughed at her friend. "Sounds like a bribe to me!"

"I'm not above bribing if it gets me a good review! Now, let me see your canvas."

"Follow me into the store," Laura said.

"Why can't I look at it outside the store, and if it fits where I want to hang it, I'll buy it from you right here?"

"That's not the way this works. Elizabeth displays my paintings, and when they sell, she gets paid for giving me a place to market my work. I would never think about cheating her out of a deal."

"Okay, okay!" Nancy muttered. "You always were one to stick to the rules."

Elizabeth looked up as the two women entered her store. "Good! You found each other. Sight unseen, Nancy seems to think that your new painting is exactly what she needs to dress up the entrance to her home."

Laura held up the canvas for them to see. "I went a little wild with this one, lots of contrasting colors. You are either going to love it or hate it on sight."

Nancy gasped. "How did you know to use those colors, Laura? It's absolutely perfect! I want to buy it right now, and I'm in a hurry." Handing Elizabeth her credit card, Nancy exclaimed, "Ring up the sale and then I'm out of here!"

Elizabeth picked up the card and looked at Laura, waiting for directions; there had been no discussion between them about the price to place upon the new painting.

"Will you please hurry?" Nancy urged. "I want to get this picture hung before anyone shows up."

Laura nodded to Elizabeth. "Price it the same as the last two that you sold."

Elizabeth wrote down the number and Nancy didn't bat an eye. "Just do it!"

Laura's disappointment in not seeing Bob was still hanging over her. She hadn't felt like this since high school.

A sudden idea made her smile. Turning to Nancy, who was twitching with impatience, she said, "I know how important this interview is to you, so you go on home, and I'll follow with the picture and hang it for you."

"Oh, Laura! What a great idea! I'll love you forever!" Nancy squealed and hugged her. Laura almost felt guilty. Her suggestion might have sounded altruistic, but it was just a ploy to get a glimpse of Bob. How high-schoolish was that?

144

Nancy signed the charge, grabbed her card, and ran out of the store.

"I think that was your quickest sale," Elizabeth remarked. "Here's a thought, Laura. Nancy has a lot of tourists coming and going all summer long. A lot of them like to take home things from the area where they vacationed. Lots of authors make their books available, so why don't we make your art available? If she would allow us, I could make an attractive sign displaying your name and directing them to my establishment where more of your work can be seen. You've been looking for a new way to market your art, and if this gets us buyers, it could be profitable for both of us."

"What a great idea!" Laura cried.

"You think Nancy will go for it?"

Laura shrugged. "We'll never know unless we ask. Nancy and I have been friends for a long time." She stopped talking as a pensive look passed over her face. "Ben and I used to do a lot of fun activities with Nancy and Mike. Now, both of us are widows."

"Is she as young as you?" Elizabeth asked.

Laura nodded. "Sudden deaths for both of them, Mike fell off the roof, and you know Ben. The accident."

"How tragic for both of you!" Elizabeth reached out and touched Laura's hand.

Laura cleared her throat; the loss of Ben was still a raw subject. To change the conversation, she declared, "Oh, in case Nancy won't have time to look for them, I think I should take a hammer and some nails with me to hang the picture."

Elizabeth reached under the counter and produced them. "Just remember to return the hammer."

Laura rushed to her car and threw the canvas, her purse, and the hammer into the back seat; the nails she tucked into her pocket. Before starting the car, she pulled down the mirrored visor and inspected her appearance. A swipe of lip-gloss, and a quick fluff with a hairbrush was all it took to assure her that all was well.

# Chapter 53

George was standing outside his shack when Nancy rushed out of the big house. A reporter and a photographer were scheduled to interview Nancy for a featured article in the Sunday's issue of the local paper.

So, where was she going? According to her schedule that she'd shared with him, he knew the delivery guy from The Hatch would be showing up within the hour. Since Nancy had already paid for the food, that wouldn't be a problem if she weren't here because he could handle that, but the reporter and photographer were another matter. One picture of him in the Sunday paper could ruin everything.

All it would take was one sharp-eyed cop who could look past his shaved head and new beard to recognize him. He had every intention to be someplace else while they were here.

Cleaning the big house and the grounds around it had kept him busy all week. When Nancy didn't have him in the house scrubbing floors, washing windows, and polishing furniture, she had him trimming shrubs, mowing the grass, and hauling trash to the dump. It pleased him to see that his old car was still there, waiting for him in case he needed a quick get-away. He'd even dug the key from its hidden place and then held his breath when he inserted the key and turned it; the engine sputtered to life on the first try.

As soon as Nancy's van was out of sight, George picked up a section of soundproofing material he had smuggled into the shack and nailed it to the wall. Nancy didn't leave home very often, and it was taking him a long time to finish the job. But there was no hurry; he hadn't even started the romantic dining and wooing of Miss Laura. He smiled just thinking about it.

At the sound of Nancy's return, he dropped the hammer and examined his work. Even though the panels were advertised as the top-of-the-line in soundproofing products, he intended to add a second layer just in case Laura caused too much of a ruckus.

When he heard what he thought must be the delivery from The Hatch, he looked out of his door and saw that it was Laura. He watched as she opened the back door of her car and struggled to remove something big from the back seat. Whatever it was, it was covered. A canvas?

Staying out of sight, he watched her as her eyes swiftly scanned the area. When they found his shack, they stopped. Was she looking for him? He waited inside until she headed for the big house. "Miss Laura," he called walking toward her. "Could I be of help?"

She stopped, and turned around. There he was, the man who had reduced a mature and sensible woman into a giggling girl with a high-school crush. What was so special about Bob Miller that turned her insides to jelly? Whatever it was, it was fun feeling like a teenager.

Greeting him with a huge smile on her face, she gushed, "Oh, hello, Bob! I was going to say no, but I changed my mind." Holding up the canvas, she added, "Do you want to help me hang this picture?"

Pointing to what she was carrying, he said, "I understand you're an artist. Is that one of yours?"

"Yes, it is!"

His eyes were shining and his smile brilliant when he looked down at her. "I'm looking forward to seeing it," he said, softly.

Laura was having trouble breathing. Being this close to Bob was intoxicating. The sun seemed to be shining brighter, the sky was cerulean, and her heart was thumping in her chest. Offering to hang the picture for Nancy was turning out to be an excellent idea.

With a chuckle, he pointed to the hammer she was carrying. "That's a vicious looking weapon you have in your hand!"

She looked up at him with seductive half-closed eyes. "The better to protect myself from the big bad wolf."

He looked around. "See any wolves? I don't."

"Just you," she grinned.

He pretended to be alarmed. "Me? A big bad wolf?" Sticking out his lower lip, he pouted. "Now, you've hurt my feelings."

She tilted her head back and laughed. "Okay, so you're not a bad guy! But you didn't answer my question."

"I forgot the question."

"No, you didn't!"

147

"Yes, I did. It's hard for me to think straight when I'm around you."

"Bob!" she laughed. "Quit teasing me! Will you help me hang the picture?"

"Oh, that's right! Of course I'll help you. I can see you have the hammer, what about nails? I don't see any nails."

"Do you think I've never hung a picture before?"

"So? Where are they?"

Laura reached into her pocket and pulled out the nails.

"Then let's get this show on the road! I want to be out of the way when the reporter and photographer arrive."

"Really? I'd think a handsome guy like you would like having his picture taken."

"So, I'm handsome now?" He reached out and playfully punched her shoulder.

"Ah, come on, Bob! You know very well that you are. So 'fess up. Why don't you like to have your picture taken?"

"I'm just not very photogenic," he shrugged. "I spoil every picture that I'm in."

"Sure you do," she scoffed. "But that's reason enough for me."

"It is?" He sounded surprised.

Laura laughed. "Come to think of it, I don't want to be in any pictures either!"

"Good! Let's hang this and then you and I can find something to do until the interview is over."

Laura almost dropped the hammer in her excitement. She was going to spend some time with Bob!

Nancy met them at the door, surprised to see her friend and Bob together. Laura was looking much too happy to suit Nancy, and a look at Bob's face didn't make her any happier. Bob was hers. She'd take this up with Laura later, but right now she needed a picture hung.

"Where does it go?" Laura asked as she removed the paper cover off the canvas.

Bob's quick intake of breath pleased her. He liked her work.

The ringing of the doorbell stopped Nancy from doing anything but point. "Right there. Hang it right there," she ordered.

148

"Please excuse me, but I have to answer the door. It better be The Hatch delivering the food and not the guys from the paper."

Bob and Laura's voices followed her as she made her way to the door. She heard Laura laugh and say, "Oh, no! You're holding it upside down!"

Nancy frowned. They were having too much fun.

# Chapter 54

Laura looked over at the man in the passenger seat of her car and secretly congratulated herself. Events just seemed to fall into place after the two of them had hung her picture in Nancy's foyer and escaped minutes before the crew from the paper arrived. For as long as the interview lasted, she had Bob all to herself. From the looks he was giving her, he was enjoying himself, too.

Once outside the house, he'd turned to her. "You know what I want to do for the next hour?"

Laura's face lit up. She tilted her head and coquettishly gazed up at him. "No, but whatever it is, I'm sure I'll enjoy it."

George had a fleeting moment of regret. For some reason, he'd been hoping that Laura would be more of a challenge than his other victims. Women were so predictable. However, he had to admit that the process of making her fall in love with him was surprisingly pleasant.

Staying in character, he smiled down at her. "Laura, I am really impressed with your work. Do you have any more finished pieces that I could see?"

The statement so surprised Laura that she stopped walking. "Really? You're serious?"

He gave her a puzzled look. "Of course I'm serious! What makes you think I wouldn't be? I really liked what I saw, Laura."

Ben had been aware of her passion for painting when he married her, but he had never paid attention to her finished canvases, nor had he encouraged her to continue painting after the birth of Teddy. To her, Bob's interest in her art was both unexpected and heartwarming.

She was having trouble holding in her sheer exuberance. Here she was, with a man who not only was extremely handsome and lots of fun, he also liked her art. How lucky she was! "That's an easy request. I have a few canvases for sale at A Touch of Color. Come on, we'll go in my car."

Elizabeth glanced up from the book she was leafing through when the door chime announced that a visitor was entering her store.

"Excuse me, Josh," she said. "I'll be right back. We need to pick a date for your book signing."

Josh Lang's first reaction when he saw a laughing Laura enter the store was to flee before the familiar scent threatened his sanity. Laura was followed in by the same guy Josh had seen her with at the diner. They stood close together, almost touching but not quite. Josh tensed up, noting the way the couple hovered around the door; he had no way to escape without being seen.

Bracing himself for the expected scent of Marie's perfume, he was caught off guard when the odor of a rotting putrid corpse filled the store. He knew the decaying smell well from research he had done for one of his books, and it was a stench that once you were exposed to it, you never forgot. He gagged.

Why wasn't Elizabeth alarmed by the odor? Laura and the guy weren't reacting to it either. Was he the only one smelling it?

Elizabeth's eyes were immediately drawn to the tall and ridiculously handsome man who followed Laura into her store. Had she already found a hunk to replace the very recently departed Ben? The thought left a sour taste in her mouth; some women have all the luck.

"Oh, there you are, Elizabeth!" Laura called. "I've brought a friend who wants to see some of my work. Elizabeth, meet Bob Miller. Bob works at Nancy's house."

Elizabeth had heard that Nancy had a new guy working for her, but no one had mentioned how handsome he was. So, he was just Laura's friend and not a lover? A relieved and hopeful Elizabeth smiled up at him alluringly and offered him her hand. "I'm Elizabeth Anderson, and welcome to A Touch of Color!"

George hid his amusement; the woman was flirting with him. Accepting her hand, he gazed into her eyes and with a warm smile. "It's so very nice to meet you, Elizabeth."

Elizabeth's heart was pounding.

Laura was not amused at what she was seeing. "We'll stay out of your way," she said, urging him to follow her away from Elizabeth. "I know where all my paintings are, and really, Mr. Miller is not a buyer."

He winked at Elizabeth as Laura dragged him past her. "Who says I'm not a buyer?"

Laura snorted. "Hang one of my creations in that shack you live in? I don't think so!"

Elizabeth's eyebrows shot up. That gorgeous man lives in a shack?

"That's only temporary, and you know it," he laughed.

Their voices faded as they made their way to where Laura's work was displayed, leaving Elizabeth disappointed that she couldn't hear their conversation. But she was sure of one thing; he definitely had reacted to her during their introduction. She needed to find out more about the guy.

After a few minutes, Laura was hustling her friend toward the door.

"But I wasn't through looking at them," he protested.

"What's the hurry?" Elizabeth asked, forgetting all about Josh Lang who was waiting for her to wrap up  the details on a book-signing event in her store.

"She claims I have to get back to work!" he chuckled. "Would you believe Laura kidnapped me?"

"Did not!"

"Did too!

Elizabeth watched them banter back and forth like kids.

Laura stopped laughing long enough to explain the situation. "Bob helped me hang the picture Nancy bought, and then she kicked us both out, told us to get lost until the interview was over."

Josh, who was watching all of this from behind a display of brushes, was holding his jacketed arm over his nose, looking ill.

Why did no one else smell it?

The awful stench grew unbearable when the guy stepped closer to inspect a piece of sculpture. Josh now knew that the smell was definitely connected to the man they were calling Bob.

"Let's go, Bob" Laura called. "I have to get you back to Nancy's and then rush home to get my kids off the bus."

Elizabeth watched them leave the store, envying the casual way Bob draped his arm around Laura's shoulders.

Josh stayed hidden behind the display, once again questioning his sanity; every trace of the malodorous and fetid stench had disappeared when the couple left the store.

"Oh, there you are, Josh," Elizabeth exclaimed when she found him pretending to be looking at the display. "I'm sorry about the interruption, but…." She stopped and looked closely at him. "Josh, are you all right? You're not looking well!"

Josh swallowed hard. "I'm fine, Elizabeth. Must be something I ate."

"Are you sure?"

He nodded, swallowing hard.

"Well, would next Saturday afternoon from noon until three o'clock fit your schedule? That will give me time to make a sign to put in my window announcing your book-signing."

Josh was so unnerved by what he'd just endured that as he drove home, he tried to remember if he'd even answered Elizabeth's question.

Maybe it was time to seek professional help?

# Chapter 56

Today. Today was the day she was going to tell Joan. The procedure had been delayed until wounds from the serial killer's attack had improved. Feeling that it was only fair that Joan should be told before it happened, today was the day.

Laura's eyes flew open, all thoughts of sleep gone, and no clue as to why the thought jarred her awake. Reaching out, she turned off the alarm that was set to go off in five minutes and then snuggled back into the warmth and softness of the bed. Just for five minutes, she told herself.

"Mom! Mom! Wake up! We're going to miss the bus!"

She jerked awake to find two sets of eyes looking down at her. "Oh," she exclaimed sitting up, "I didn't mean to go back to sleep! Get dressed, and I'll go downstairs and start breakfast."

"But Mom! You always pick out what we're going to wear," Beth reminded her.

She grabbed her robe and while putting it on, she yelled over her shoulder, "Surprise me today, the both of you. Now get going."

The children slid into their seats just as she placed toast and oatmeal on the table. Trying to keep a straight face, she looked at their choices. Nothing matched, one shirt was on backward, and one was inside out. By the time they heard the bus approaching, all clothing problems had been corrected, teeth had been brushed, and Laura breathed a sigh of relief as Teddy and Beth ran to join their friends at the bus stop.

Two hours later, Laura pulled into the parking lot of the Rehab Center and shut off the motor. She sat and thought about what she was about to do. In her heart, she felt that her friend deserved to be told that she was pregnant even if John didn't want her to know. It was on her shoulder that Joan cried as year after year of trying never ended in pregnancy. Laura knew that John didn't have an inkling as to how far Joan had gone in her search for the special sperm that would give her a baby.

Whoa! There was no guard outside Joan's room! Laura rushed down the hall and into the room, only to come to an abrupt halt when she saw an empty bed.

The receptionist looked up as Joan's daily visitor ran up to her desk. "If you're looking for Joan, she's in the hospital."

"The hospital?" Laura gasped. "Did something happen to her?"

The woman shrugged. "For that information, you'll have to talk to Dr. Daily."

"Is she in?"

"Yes, she is. I'll call and see if she'll see you."

After a short conversation, she ended the call. "Do you remember how to find Dr. Daily's office?"

Laura nodded. "Yes, I do, and thank you."

Dr. Daily met Laura at the door. "Come in and have a seat," she said. "You are not going to like what's happening."

Laura's eyes widened. "Why? Did something bad happen? Is she alright?"

"If you think aborting her baby without her knowledge is wrong, then yes, something bad is happening to her."

"Right now? It's happening right now?"

Dr. Daily nodded. "We both knew that John had the last say in the situation, and he was adamant about aborting the fetus, so it was bound to happen."

"I knew that, but as Joan's friend, I felt she had the right to be told, and that's what I was going to do today. She hasn't reacted to anything I've said so far, but I was hoping that her hearing that she was pregnant would get a response out of her." Laura paused, wondering if she should continue this line of conversation. "Maybe I'm out of line, but I'm going to tell you what lengths she has gone in her effort to conceive. Would you believe that Joan, my best friend, seduced my husband?"

Dr. Daily gasped. "And you're still her friend?"

"And I watched her crawl into George Knox's truck, hoping that having sex with the handsome killer posing as a flower delivery man would result in a pregnancy. That's how the serial killer got his hands on her. And yes, I'm still her friend."

Dr. Daily sat quietly for a moment. "That's quite a story. I'm surprised, though, that she chose your husband."

"I'm partly to blame for that. Joan loves my two children, and I can't count how many times I've told her how great it would be if she had a Teddy and a Beth of her own. In her twisted thinking, she reasoned that in order to have a Teddy and a Beth of her own, she needed the same sperm donor, and that would be Ben, my husband. To her, it made so much sense that she was even astonished that I got upset when I found out."

"I'm not surprised. There's no limit as to how far a woman obsessed with having a baby will go to get one," Dr. Daily mused. "I'm remembering a patient some years ago who was referred to me after she was caught in the hospital's maternity ward trying to steal a newborn."

Laura grimaced. "I guess we should be glad that Joan only stole husbands and not babies."

"And you, Laura. Did your marriage survive your husband's betrayal?"

"That was a decision that I never had to make," she said lightly. "Ben ran a red light, and an eighteen-wheeler truck took care of it."

"He's dead?" Dr. Daily's raised eyebrows showed surprise at the openly hostile statement. Laura may have forgiven Joan, but she sure hadn't forgiven Ben.

Laura nodded.

Dr. Daily placed one of her cards on the desk. "Here's how to reach me if you ever want to talk about it."

Laura picked up the card and studied it. She liked talking to Dr. Daily, and maybe someday she'd look her up.

"I guess we're finished here, but before I go, I have a question. Would there be any reason now to tell Joan that John took away her one chance to have a baby?"

Dr. Daily shook her head. "No reason at all. What's done is done, and let's let that be the end of it."

"Thank you, Dr. Daily."

Laura was walking with her head down thinking about how tragic it was that the much-wanted fetus was being aborted and almost missed seeing Bob going into Joan's room.

By the time she neared Joan's room, Bob, whose sweet face was now contorted into a fierce and angry scowl, was coming out of it. The ferociousness of it scared her. Where was the caring and loveable Bob that she was accustomed to seeing? Scared, Laura held her breath as he came toward her. How was she going to greet him? Could she pretend that she hadn't seen anything? Yes, that was it. Play dumb, and maybe he'd tell her what was so upsetting in the empty room. With a fixed smile on her face she waited for him to reach her, only to watch him walk right past her heading in the direction of the exit door. He was going to leave without saying anything?

"Bob! Bob!" she called out.

He turned, and the scary and fierce unfamiliar face morphed into the kind and loveable Bob that she knew.

"Oh, Laura! I didn't see you!"

"Really? You walked right past me!"

"You have to forgive me. I was just so upset that, uh, you know, uh, well, I was just so upset that your friend Joan wasn't in her room that I wasn't thinking of anything else."

Her eyes questioned his remark. "Really? Why would that be so upsetting to you? You don't even know her."

*Damn nosey cunt!* "I was upset because, ah, because I knew how worried you must be!"

"What?"

He bowed his head, paused for a moment for effect, then looked into her eyes. "Laura, there's something you don't know about me."

She took a step away from him.

"Oh!" he laughed. "It's nothing bad."

"That's good to know! You sounded so serious, I thought for a minute there you were going to confess to being a serial killer."

The smile on his face disappeared.

She reached out her hand to him. "Come on, Bob! Please tell me what it is that I don't know about you."

*The bitch is going to eat those words one of these days.* "I've been plagued with this problem all my life. I guess I just care too much. When any friend of mine has a problem, I take it on as if it were my own." He stopped to sigh.

"And?" Laura asked when he didn't continue. "You still haven't told me why you were so upset when you came out of Joan's room. Bob, I saw your face, and it was scary."

"I can only imagine how I looked, and I'm sorry that you had to see it." He lowered his eyes, then looked up at her. "Laura, I have felt from the beginning that God wanted me to pray for your friend even though she is unresponsive. He was leading me into her room the day you stopped me, and although I should have been stronger, I allowed you to do it. Today when I listened to Him and went into her room and found it empty, I knew that I'd let Him down. You have no idea how upset I was with myself."

George was intently studying Laura. Had he pulled it off? Joan's empty bed had been a shock. Just the thought that he might be denied the chance to finish his kill had sent him into instant fury. Laura still had an uneasy look about her that George didn't like. He needed to do something big right now to divert her attention away from his slip-up.

His face broke into a big smile. "I'm so glad that I ran into you! Nancy doesn't have anything for me to do, and until now, I had no plans for the day. But seeing you here all dressed up and looking so pretty, I have two great ideas."

Laura's concerned face changed in an instant. "What did you have in mind?"

"Oh, for one thing, my stomach tells me it's time to eat. How does lunch sound?"

He held his breath, hoping he'd smoothed over his blunder. Until he was finished with Joan, he couldn't let Laura become suspicious. He wasn't through with her yet.

"Lunch is a great idea," she replied, relieved that her sweet Bob was back. "And the second idea?"

"An early movie that will get you back before your kids come home! I don't have any idea what's playing right now, so we both can be surprised."

158

Gazing into his brown eyes, she quickly forgot any doubts about him. Bob and his kind heart! She had wrongly interpreted the look on his face. And then she remembered Joan.

"Tell you what. I'll accept the lunch offer because I'm really hungry, but I'll take a rain check on the movie. I want to spend the afternoon with Joan."

Instant fury hit. Damn Joan and her interference! It took extreme effort to keep his face from registering his feelings. Instead, he leaned in and kissed Laura softly on her cheek. "A rain check? You've got it."

Laura's feet wanted to skip as they headed toward the exit door. A lunch with Bob! "Shall we take my car?"

He stopped walking. "That's a good idea, but before we go, let's ask about Joan at the front desk. There has to be a reason she's not in her room."

"No need to, Bob. I know where she is."

His face suddenly contorted with rage. He raised one hand as if to strike her, while his other hand roughly grabbed her shoulder. Pulling her close, he placed his forehead against hers and sinisterly hissed. "You knew and didn't tell me? You saw how upset I was!"

Stunned, surprised, and scared by Bob's unexpected anger, she pulled away and stammered, "Y-y-you didn't ask."

Lowering his raised hand, he rubbed his bald head, hoping that she'd believe that's all he ever intended to do. He took a deep breath, relaxed his face, and regained his sweet Bob mask. God, how long could he go on with this charade? Sweet Bob made him want to puke.

"Oh, you must forgive me!" he apologized, removing his hands from her shoulders. "It's just that I care so very much that sometimes," he stopped to sniffle and wipe at a non-existent tear, "my emotions just get away from me. So tell me, where is she?"

Something wasn't right. What was that old saying that if someone seems too good to be true, he probably isn't? She stepped back, and took a good look at him. His face was smiling now, but she'd seen another side of Bob that was downright frightening.

Disappointment hit hard; Bob Miller wasn't the man she thought he was. In a flat voice she informed him, "Right now, Joan's baby is being aborted. She's in the hospital."

"No!" he yelled. "They can't do that!"

"Bob, lower your voice! There are patients in all these rooms!"

He bowed his head. "Sorry!"

"Of course they can proceed, because that's what her husband wants. And by now, the procedure is probably finished."

Instant fury flared again. How dare they kill his baby! It was his to decide what happened to it! Laura's gasp cut through his rage. Damn! Quickly, he turned his face away from her, but not quick enough.

Laura's heart was pounding and her instinct told her to run. How could she have been so gullible? Ben was barely cold in his grave, and here she was being dazzled by a man who had showed up out of nowhere, pretending to be somebody who he wasn't.

Giving him her biggest smile, she hit the back of her hand on her forehead. "Oh, silly me! Your wonderful invitation of lunch and a movie made me forget! I have an appointment with my lawyer that I'm already late for. He's so busy that I've had to wait weeks to get into see him." Stepping around him, she called over her shoulder as she rushed to the exit door. "Maybe next time?"

# Chapter 57

With a resigned sigh, Josh raked his fingers through his hair, hit the delete key, and watched the paragraph he'd spent the last hour writing disappear from his computer screen. If he couldn't do any better than that, he should quit trying.

Hoping to see something that would give him an idea for his next book, he walked to the window and looked out. Unfortunately, all he saw was the reflection in the glass of a man who needed a shave and a haircut. His hair poked about in different directions, making him look more porcupine than human. The last time he'd had a writing block he'd stood at this very same window and watched a canoeist paddle toward the other side of the lake. The plot line had materialized out of nowhere and the chapters appeared on the computer screen as if written by someone else. The book had been a success, as always. Why couldn't it happen again? Where was that spark?

The cabin was snug and warm, thanks to adding insulation and installing baseboard heat, but it was too quiet. The only human sound his ears heard was his own voice when he read a newly written chapter aloud. But then, he would delete it and stare at the blinking cursor some more. Was he wrong in insisting that this story line was going to be different from all his other books?

He shook his head, clearing his mind. If he wanted a different story line, he had to figure out where to get one. Without something tangible to present, his publisher wasn't happy when Josh shared his plan to write something new. Why change a winning formula, the publisher kept asking? Because I'm bored, Josh kept answering.

The end result wasn't good. Heated words were exchanged when the publisher refused to give him advance money for the book and no guarantee that when it was finished, his company would even publish it. Now, just like every other author in the world, Josh was on his own, and he didn't like the feeling. Maybe his publisher was right; maybe it was a bad idea.

Writing was his profession, the only skill he had to make a living. If he couldn't write anymore, how was he going to survive? His last book was still at the top of a few charts so money wasn't a problem, but if his next book didn't get published, he'd soon be in financial trouble.

Turning away from the window, he surveyed his little cabin that right now felt more like a prison cell. He needed to get out and mix with people. His stomach growled, giving him the perfect excuse to mingle with society.

The newly opened Flamingo Bar and Grill was doing a brisk luncheon business when Josh arrived. The owner must have thought that if one flamingo lawn ornament was good, many more would be better, because they seemed to be everywhere.

A waitress appeared immediately, took his beverage order, and left him with a menu that had a picture of a flamingo on the front of it. Josh decided that if baked, broiled, or fried flamingo appeared on the menu, he'd leave.

He was studying his choices when a faint smell of garbage made him lower the menu. Scanning the restaurant, he quickly spotted the man he'd seen last Sunday at the art studio. Josh was still studying the man when the unmistakable stench of rotting flesh hit his nose.

The urge to vomit sent Josh rushing out of the restaurant right past the surprised waitress who was bringing his coffee. Once he made it outside, he leaned against the side of the building and gulped fresh air into his lungs. What the hell was going on? Obviously, he was the only one who smelled the stench, but how could that be? Why him? Why were all these unexplainable things happening to him?

Wait a minute! Josh's face broke into a grin. Unusual happenings, mystery, romance, perfume, garbage, music…paranormal!

He had just stumbled upon the genre for his next book.

# Chapter 58

Nancy was putting an overnight case into her car when she looked up and saw Bob standing outside his shed.

"Good morning, Bob!" she called.

Walking toward her, he called back, "Going somewhere?"

"I was going to tell you before I left. There are no tenants right now, and since I hadn't visited my mother in months, I figured this was a good time to do it."

"How long will you be gone?"

"Oh, just one night. I'll leave the 'No Vacancy' sign on until I return tomorrow, probably around noon."

George waved to her as she drove off, trying to hold back the excitement that was bubbling inside him. This was the opportunity he'd been waiting for. He was prepared for what he was going to do, he just didn't know how he was going to pull it off. Nancy's leaving was truly a bit of luck.

It was time to close the Joan deal. His inability to reign in his anger had ruined his plan to wine, dine, and woo Laura until she fell in love with him. It wasn't going to happen. He was disappointed because it was so much more fulfilling to torture someone who was in love with him.

George went into his shack and gathered the bags that were full of clothes that he'd bought at a resale store several towns away. Using his key, he entered Nancy's house and went directly to her bathroom where he shaved off his beard, applied Nancy's make-up to his face, and put a long, dark brown wig over his shaved head. Next, he went to her bedroom in search of a full-length mirror.

Out of the bags he pulled women's clothes with tags that were marked extra-extra-large, and because he couldn't find a pair of woman's shoes to fit his big feet, he'd settled for sandals with open toes.

Standing in front of the mirror, he studied the reflection of a large but rather attractive woman. Could he pull this off? The guard was the problem. His original plan was to find a way to lure the guard away from Joan's door, but there was no time for that now. However, the guard had been leaving his post more often lately, but not on a regular schedule. If he were lucky, he would be in and out without running into anyone, and it wouldn't take long to do away with Joan.

George took the van back to the dump and switched it for his stolen car. As he pulled into the Rehab Center parking lot, he made one last check of his appearance before he crawled out of the car, straightened his dress, and headed off to finish the Joan project once and for all.

Good. No one was at the reception desk, the hall to Joan's room was clear, and there wasn't a guard by her door. George gloated, accepting all the good things that were happening.

Joan didn't react when he entered her room. Her dead eyes kept staring at the wall even as he hovered over her holding a pillow.

"Hello, Joan," he crooned as he lowered the pillow. "We meet again, if only briefly."

That voice! The violence that she associated with it exploded in her sealed off mind. Joan came to life, filled her lungs with air and screamed while nails that hadn't been tended to in a long time reached up and raked the skin off his hands.

Blood! George looked down at his bleeding hands in horror. The little cunt was supposed to be comatose! He could hear pounding feet coming toward her room, probably the guard returning to his post. Before Joan could scream again, he dropped the bloody pillow and ran from the room. He could hear the guard ordering him to stop as he ran past the still empty reception desk and out into the parking lot. He was still shaking when he reached the dump.

# Chapter 59

"It was him!" Joan sobbed. "That voice! I'll never forget that voice!"

Laura held her violently shaking friend. "But the guard keeps insisting that it was a woman who ran out of your room."

"I don't care what the guard says! It was George Knox! Believe me, it was him!" Joan begged.

Laura rocked Joan as if she were a baby. "The guard lost his job. Did you know that?"

"I never knew there was a guard outside my door," Joan marveled. "There's so much I didn't know, Laura. I was just too scared to come out of my little safe cocoon, but he found me anyway."

John rushed into the room. "Oh, Joan!" he cried. "You're awake! Thank God you came back to me!"

Joan opened her arms. "Come here. I know you were with me most of the time. I could feel you, I just couldn't talk to you."

Laura moved off the bed to allow John to embrace his wife.

"I feel so safe when you hold me, John. But he's still out there!" Joan sobbed. "Why does he feel he needs to kill me?"

Laura opened her mouth to tell her what Dr. Zumwalt had said, but closed it. Joan didn't need to hear that in the deranged mind of George Knox, the demons that made him attack her in the first place wouldn't be satisfied until he ended it.

Laura backed out of the room, giving Joan and John some private time. As she walked to her car, her mind went back again to her conversation with Dr. Zumwalt. When he was explaining George Knox's obsession with blond long-legged women, he'd stated, "You do know that you fit that description, don't you?"

A sharp stab of fear left her breathless. In her mind's eye, she remembered the killer standing on her porch, a bouquet of flowers in his hand while he watched Joan crawl into his truck. He knew where she lived!

Laura laid her head on the steering wheel and shuddered. Where could she and her children go? Her mind raced; who would take them in? Elizabeth? But then she remembered that Elizabeth lived in a one-bedroom apartment. She pounded the wheel in frustration. Think! She had to think, but stark terror was scrambling her thoughts. What about Teddy and Beth? Were they in danger, too? Wait a minute! She could stay in her house if she had someone living there to protect her and her children. But who?

Bob?

The idea slowed down her breathing. There was something about Bob that scared her, but he certainly wasn't a serial killer. Maybe she had judged him too harshly. Should she give him another chance? The sudden recall of the evil she'd seen in his face made her shiver. No, Bob was never going to get close to her kids. But you couldn't say that he wasn't special. His Bible study group at church was thriving, and remembering Ida Fox taking her first step after his healing prayer at the Rehab Center still gave her chills. Her thoughts were interrupted by the sound of her cell-phone ringing deep inside her purse. When her searching hand finally found it, she saw that it was a call from Nancy.

"Hello?"

"Laura, it's Nancy."

"I know," Laura answered. "What's up?"

"Well, I'm worried about you."

"You are?"

"Yes. Ever since I heard what the serial killer tried to do to Joan. Laura, if George Knox is back in this area, he's probably looking for another tall blond woman, and that description definitely fits you."

Laura groaned. "I'm sitting in my car in the parking lot of the Rehab Center thinking the same thing. He knows where I live, Nancy."

"He does? That's not good!"

"I can't think of a place that's safe for me and my children. I don't know where to go! And I'm scared!"

Nancy took a deep breath. Did she really want to do this? Bob was hers, but she had seen that Laura had feelings for him, too. Why should she make it easy for them to be together? But if she didn't and something happened to Laura, she'd never forgive herself. "What would you think about coming here and staying in one of my cabins

166

until we're sure the serial killer is out of our area? The tourist season is over, and I have a lot of vacancies."

"Oh, Nancy! You would do that for me?"

"That's what friends are for, Laura."

"Thank you, thank you, thank you!" Laura cried. "The children and I will be over after they get home from school this afternoon. I'm going home right now to pack our bags. Nancy, I owe you big time for doing this!"

Nancy really was a good friend. Now would be a good time to ask her if she'd let her and Elizabeth advertise her paintings.

And as for George Knox, he was going to have a hard time finding her.

# Chapter 60

"Bob?" Nancy listened for a sign of life inside the shack. Hearing none, she gave a tentative knock on the door. "Bob? Are you in there?"

*Damn nosy woman!* George grumbled. He groaned in response.

Nancy gasped. "Something wrong? Bob, talk to me. Are you all right?"

Making his voice weak and gravely, he replied, "No, I'm not!"

"Are you ill?"

He sneezed, coughed, and blew his nose. "It's just," he paused for another sneeze, "it's probably just a cold, but I'm feeling pretty awful."

"Oh, I'm so sorry! So, that's why you missed breakfast and lunch. Will you be able to have dinner with me and four of the guests?"

George moaned.

"That bad? Then could I bring you something? You have to be starving!"

George could hear his stomach agreeing with her. "Uh," he croaked, "now that you've offered, a little hot soup would feel good on my sore throat."

"Oh, you poor thing! You sound awful."

He paused in a series of fake coughs. "Nancy?"

"Yes, Bob?"

"I'm pretty contagious right now and probably will be for the next couple of days. So, when you bring the food, just knock on my door, and then leave it."

"You are something else, Bob," she chuckled. "Even when you're ill, you still look out for the rest of us. Tell me, can your throat handle crackers with the soup?"

George's mouth watered. "I'll manage. I'm really hungry."

George ran his hand over his bristly face as he listened to the sound of her footsteps fading away. Not only had he stayed away from

168

the big house for meals, he'd stayed away from Nancy's bathroom, too. The woods behind the shack was getting a workout.

He'd shaved off his beard for the Joan fiasco, and until it grew enough to cover his face, he had to stay hidden. Unfortunately, his shaved head was also growing a five o'clock shadow, and although he didn't have a mirror, he knew that he was looking more like George Knox than Bob Miller. At least while he played the invalid, he didn't have to wear the bothersome brown contacts. Sticking his finger into his eye to put in a foreign object just didn't seem natural. He had no way of knowing if Nancy has seen his wanted posters, but until his beard grew in, he wasn't taking any chances. Once that happened, he'd use Nancy's bathroom to take a much-needed shower and shave his head.

Nancy was true to her word, and thirty minutes later she knocked on his door. "Bob? The soup and coffee are really hot, so be careful. I also made you a sandwich, but if your throat is too sore to eat it, that's okay."

"Nancy," he paused to cough. "Thank you. You are being so kind."

"You're welcome, Bob. I'm so sorry you're not feeling well. And Bob?"

"Yes?"

"I'll bring your breakfast in the morning, too."

Cough, cough. "Bless you! And Nancy, could you bring water, too?"

"Of course! I should have thought of that. In fact, I'll bring some over after I clean up the dinner mess."

He waited until he heard the door on the big house close before he stepped outside and picked up his dinner.

Once inside, George stumbled around in the dark windowless shack searching for a place to spread the food. He'd been asking Nancy for more candles because he was down to his last one, but finding that one candle and matches in the inky blackness of the shack was impossible. Since it was just late afternoon, all he had to do was open the door and enough light from outside would come in and help him in the search.

With the tray balanced with one hand, he opened the door with his other one…and almost dropped everything. Getting out of a car was his Laura and her two kids. Knowing that the two women were friends, he wasn't surprised that Laura was visiting Nancy, but why were the kids carrying overnight cases? The mystery deepened when Laura opened the trunk and started removing additional suitcases.

Before she could look over and see him, he backed up and quietly pulled the door shut. What were they doing here? Thank God, the shack didn't have any windows for her to peek in! He'd have to wait for Nancy to bring the water to find out.

It was surprising how much light just one little candle threw into his small shack. George finished his meager meal, wiped his face on his sleeve, and looked around his shack that suddenly felt like a prison. Nothing to read, and with only the wax-dripping candle to watch, claustrophobia was starting to gnaw at him. This was all Joan's fault! Why was she making it so hard for him? She was supposed to be dead, and not in a guarded room. To finish the Joan project, he'd shaved off his beard and now he had to sit in this shitty little shack with nothing to do.

The closed in feeling was being replaced by a low simmering rage. So what if the Joan project was unfinished and the plan to make Laura fall in love with him hadn't worked? Setbacks never stopped him before, and they weren't going to stop him now. Laura was his. It was just a matter of time.

But first, his beard had to regrow to cover the dimple in both of his cheeks that stood out so prominently in the damn wanted posters. He was wondering just how long he could claim contagiousness for hiding out when he heard Nancy's knock.

"Bob?"

"Hi, Nancy. Bringing me water?"

"Yes, and a little snack, too. I made some pudding that will slide right down your sore throat. Hey, you're sounding better!"

Damn! He'd forgotten to act sick. A cough and a sneeze later, he exclaimed in a gruff voice, "No such luck."

"Well, enjoy the pudding."

"Nancy, could I ask you a question?"

"Of course, Bob."

"I happened to look out and saw Laura and her two kids. Are they visiting you?"

"Oh, my! You've been cooped up so you haven't heard the latest! You'll never believe what happened to our friend, Joan. You know, the one who escaped from the serial killer? Well, he found her again!"

"No!"

"Yes!" Nancy exclaimed. "Bob, that evil man is back in this area!"

"No!"

"Yes, he is! You'd think he'd be far away after what he did to our friend, but apparently not, because he showed up at the Rehab Center dressed like a woman and tried to kill her! Can you believe that?"

"And they didn't catch him?"

"No, and the guard lost his job because he wasn't sitting outside Joan's door when it happened. It kinda makes you feel sorry for the guard, doesn't it? Why, how long did they expect him to sit there without a bathroom break? Don't you think they should have thought of that before they pulled the other guard off? Goodness, sometimes no one uses good common sense these days. Have you thought that, too?"

Nancy was making him appreciate the silence of his shack.

"I noticed that your visitors brought suitcases with them. Will they be staying long?"

Nancy whispered as if she were telling him a secret. "Bob, have you paid attention to Laura?"

"Paid attention? What do you mean?"

"I mean paid attention to her appearance?"

"Why, yes. She's very attractive, as I remember."

"Did you notice that she is blond and has very long legs?"

"Yes. That's pretty hard to miss. What are you getting at?"

"Why the serial killer, of course! Haven't you heard that he only chooses tall blonds to kill?"

"Seems to me that I heard that somewhere," he said, trying to keep the amusement out of his gruff voice.

"So, that's why Laura and her kids are going to stay with me until we're sure that evil George Knox has left our area. Oh, Bob! I feel so much safer with you here to protect us!"

George's mouth was still hanging open when Nancy bid him good night and left.

# Chapter 61

Josh was on a roll. All he had to do was tie up some loose ends in his story and the book, *Essence*, would be finished. He was so sure he'd written a bestseller that he'd already sent excerpts of it to other publishers. Since he was a proven moneymaking author, several had sent back contracts. Just wait until his old publisher finds out! It was going to be fun to watch him eat his words.

His fingers were flying over the keys when they typed a question for one of the characters.

"So tell me. Why do I always smell my wife's perfume whenever I get near you?"

Josh's fingers stopped typing. Up until now, nothing had hindered the steady flow of words that was creating his story. Unlike any of his other books, this one was filled with unexplained happenings, unaccountable smells, and music that seemed to appear out of thin air.

An hour later, Josh was still at his computer but he wasn't writing. In desperation, he reread his story, hoping a clue would jump out at him. That's when the truth hit, and it hit hard; he had no idea what was going on in either his story or his own life.

Days went by, and his fingers refused to type. Interested publishers who had been told that the book was almost finished were making inquiries. Where was the great novel that Josh had bragged about?

It was becoming clear that to finish the book, he had to first get to the bottom of his own mystery.

It had all started the day he rescued the drowning woman.

He needed to talk to Laura Baker.


The sound of the dull and rusty drill cutting through two layers of soundproofing material and the shack's wooden wall shattered the silence in the pitch-black shack; his one lonely candle had burned itself out. Nancy had no more to give him, and without a beard to cover his dimples, he couldn't go shopping.

George laid down the drill, brushed away the debris and placed his right eye over the hole. Stir-crazy from too many days holed up in a shack with no windows, the need to see the light of day was making him desperate. And how many more days could he stay out of sight claiming his cold was contagious? He could only feel his beard and wonder what it really looked like, and his shaved head probably resembled a Chia Pet. It was a good thing that somewhere in the shack he had a ballcap he could wear when he finally walked out the door and into Nancy's bathroom. With a few more drilled holes, maybe he'd have enough light to find the hat.

All was quiet on the outside. It didn't look as if any of Nancy's cabins were occupied except for the one that Laura's car was parked by. The two layers of soundproofing in his shack had kept him from hearing the outside world. Even though he was satisfied with his handiwork, he was becoming increasingly agitated.

Tires crunching the gravel driveway got his attention. Keeping his eye at the hole, he watched one of the guys from church crawl out of his car. Someone had told him that the man was a writer who lived on the other side of the lake. Josh something. He was a crabby loner, who only stayed up this way during the warmer months.

He watched him enter Nancy's house, only to reappear with her moments later; together they walked to Laura's cabin. When they disappeared inside, he chose another spot and drilled.

# Chapter 62

Laura stepped back from the door to make room for her visitors. "You'll have to pardon the mess!" She pointed to the easel standing in the middle of the small room. "I'll just move it to the corner. I wasn't expecting company!"

"I wasn't expecting company either," Nancy exclaimed, "but Josh Lang showed up at my door asking to see you. Do you know him, Laura?"

Laura faced Josh, her smile tentative. "You want to see me?"

"Yes, I do. We need to talk," he answered, quietly.

Laura shrugged. "Usually, you take off running in the opposite direction when you see me. So, what's changed?"

"You need to hear the reason why just seeing you makes me doubt my sanity," he answered.

Stunned, Laura backed away from him.

"So, you do know him!" Nancy exclaimed.

"Yes," Laura answered, her eyes still fixed on Josh. "He saved my life."

Nancy's eyebrows rose. "He did what?"

Laura motioned to her guests. "Please, both of you sit. I just brewed a pot of tea. Would either of you care for a cup?"

Both nodded.

While Laura was fixing a tray, Josh stepped to the easel and studied the picture. "I know that cottage!" he exclaimed. "Laura, I'm impressed! I can almost smell the flowers growing around the white picket fence!"

"Why, thank you, Josh! I do commission work for A Spot of Color."

"That's right! You were going to paint a picture of the cottage for my wife, but she died before you even started."

Nancy interrupted. "I'm dying of curiosity, you two! How did he save your life?"

"He saved me from drowning, and I've been wanting to thank him ever since, but I never had the opportunity." Turning to Josh, Laura took his hand and squeezed it. "Josh, I thank you, from the bottom of my heart, thank you!"

He grinned at her and bowed. "It was my pleasure, ma'am."

Nancy's agitation was growing. "Is anyone ever going to tell me anything?"

Josh waited until everyone had their tea. "Laura, I need to tell the story because unexplainable things started to happen that day."

Intrigued, Laura set down her cup and slid to the edge of the chair.

"I should have been arranging my wife's funeral, but for some reason, I got it in my head that Marie would want her shadowbox to be buried with her. The box contained sand from our beach and rocks that we picked up on our walks. The trouble was that the box was here at our cottage, a five-hour drive away. It didn't make sense, but the urge was too strong to fight; I felt that I had to do it." He stopped to sip his tea. "The shadowbox always sat on the fireplace mantle, but when I finally got to the cottage, it wasn't there. My heart sank. I thought I driven all this way for nothing. Then, from our bedroom came the smell of Marie's perfume. Now, her perfume is distinctive because she'd found a site on the Internet that helped her design her own scent. She had been ill for a long time, and since the trip to the cottage was too much for her, she hadn't been here at the lake for over a year. But there on the bedside table was the shadowbox and beside it, an upset bottle of her perfume." He stopped, took a deep breath, and continued. "I felt her presence; it was so strong, I collapsed onto our bed. Believe me when I say she was there!" Savoring the moment, he briefly closed his eyes, and then opened them to continue. "When I recovered, I noticed that the bottle of perfume was standing upright and unopened. Now, I'm a rational man and things like this don't happen to me. I was doubting my senses. That's when the curtain on the window facing the lake moved, and it kept moving until I went to the window and looked out. Someone was drowning."

Laura gasped. "If you hadn't returned for the shadowbox, you wouldn't have been there to save me!"

"But Marie made sure I was there," Josh replied, quietly.

Nancy's mouth was hanging open.

"I started the motorboat and rushed to the swimmer. As I got close, I shut off the motor and paddled toward the person who was trying to stay afloat while humming a very familiar song. It was our song, and had been since the first time Marie and I met."

"I don't remember doing that!" Laura whispered.

"Well, you did. When I got you in the boat, you were scared and shivering, so I put my shirt around your shoulders. That's when I smelled Marie's perfume on you."

"Now, I do remember that! You demanded to know why I was wearing your wife's perfume!"

Josh nodded. "And that was just the beginning."

"The beginning of what?" Laura asked.

He turned and studied her face. "Laura, who are you? Why did Marie want me to save you? And why do I smell her perfume every time I see you?"

Laura's cup rattled on the saucer. "What?"

"It's true. I even saw you in one of her coats."

"No, no! You couldn't have!"

"But I did! You were coming to one of my book signing events, and I saw you! Not only did I smell the perfume on you, you were wearing one of her coats that I'd taken to the resale store."

Laura was stunned. "Yes, I did buy a coat there!"

"Do you blame me for running? The curtain, the song, the perfume, and the coat were just too much."

"You are sitting beside me. Do you smell her perfume now?"

He shook his head. "No, I don't."

The three sat in silence for several minutes. Laura finally broke the silence. "Tell me about Marie."

Josh shrugged. "Marie was the love of my life. I really didn't want to go on living after she died." He stopped and took a deep breath. "Laura, there's something about you that reminds me of her. The coloring is wrong, but the way you move, your gestures, your voice…" he stopped to swallow a sob.

"What is her background?" Laura asked, trying to ignore Josh's emotions.

He threw up his hands. "That's a story all by itself! We tried for many years to fill in the blanks, but we came up with nothing more than what was in the police report." He stopped to take a sip of his lukewarm tea.

Nancy couldn't take it anymore. "For God's sake, Josh! Don't stop now! What was in the report?"

Josh had a faraway look in his eye, remembering the letter. "Marie was just a few weeks old when she was abandoned at an adoption agency. There was a letter pinned to her blanket. It was written by the person who delivered her at the scene of a fatal car accident. Upon seeing that the parents were dead, the person had taken her. You would think that a missing newborn from a traffic accident would leave behind some kind of record, but a nationwide search came up with no such case."

Laura didn't realize that she was holding her breath until it escaped her lungs with a tortured sound.

"H..h..how old would Marie be if she hadn't died?" Laura was having trouble talking.

"Her birthday is next month, and it would have been her thirtieth."

Nancy watched as the color drained from Laura's face. "Laura? Are you alright?"

Tears were streaming down her face as she swayed back and forth moaning, "I don't believe it!"

"Laura!" Nancy yelled, worried. "What don't you believe?"

Josh went to the kitchen and came back with a paper towel. "Here, Laura. Sorry, I couldn't find a Kleenex."

Laura wiped her eyes and cleared her throat. "Thirty years ago next month, I was delivered at the site of an accident by a Good Samaritan. When the police arrived, they found me next to my dead parents who had no identification on them. The car had been stolen, so with nothing to work with, I never found out who my parents were, or where I came from. I was adopted by a wonderful family, so once I got older I stopped looking."

"No!" breathed Nancy.

Laura's voice was flat. "It's true."

Too full of emotion to talk, Josh just sat and raked his hands through his hair.

"What are you thinking, Josh?" Laura finally asked.

"You and Marie are twins! The Good Samaritan, if that's what you'd call this person, took one baby and left the other. That has to be the connection between the two of you. Marie is trying to tell me something, but what?"

Nancy's face lit up. "Maybe she's trying to get the two of you together because she doesn't want you to be alone."

Josh and Laura locked eyes, and then they both shook their heads.

"Then what?" Josh wondered. When his question was met with silence, he knew it was time to reveal another piece of the puzzle. "Nancy, what do you know about Bob?"

Nancy looked puzzled. "You mean Bob Miller, the guy living in my shack?"

"Yes. Have you ever wondered why it's taking so long for parts to be shipped? And where is the garage that has the car?"

"W…why Bob is the sweetest guy I've ever met! He can quote from the Bible and, and…."

"But do you know anything about him?"

Laura interrupted Josh. "Why are you changing the subject? I have a million questions to ask about Marie and you want to talk about Bob?"

Josh paused before he answered. "When I see you, I smell perfume. When I see Bob, I smell a rotting putrid corpse."

Laura gasped, and Nancy looked horrified.

"No, no! That can't be!" Nancy moaned. "My Bob is wonderful!"

"Your Bob?" Laura poked Nancy in the ribs. "Now he's your Bob?"

"Ladies! Knock it off!" Josh yelled. "Let's figure this out. I think that Marie is telling me that Bob is evil."

Nancy sniffed. "Evil? I don't believe it."

Laura's face brightened. "I just remembered that last Sunday at the omelet shop I was sitting next to Bob when I caught you looking at us. The next thing I saw was you running out of the restaurant as if someone were chasing you."

Josh opened his mouth to tell them about how Bob's eyes had turned into devil eyes, but changed his mind. "I was running because Marie's perfume was so strong it was making me ill."

"Bob was there, too. Did you smell bad things then?"

"No, that time I just smelled perfume. But do you remember the day you and Bob went into A Touch of Color?"

Laura nodded.

"I was there, in the back. Elizabeth and I were coming up with a date for me to have a book signing in her store. When the two of you came in, that's when I smelled the stench of death. Bob went to examine a sculpture, and the closer he got to me, the stronger the smell became. There's no doubt that the stench was coming from him."

Nancy was shaking her head. "This can't be true. Why, Bob is one of the most caring souls I've ever met! Come on, Laura, you even saw him heal Ida Fox!"

Laura didn't say anything. She hadn't forgotten how sweet Bob had turned into a very scary Bob that day at the Rehab Center.

Nancy was getting upset. "I don't believe any of this! Maybe Marie thinks that Bob Miller is not a good man, but I think she's wrong, and I bet that Laura thinks so, too."

"Not after what I saw at the Rehab Center."

Josh's head whipped around. "What did you see?"

"I had agreed to spend the afternoon with him, and I'm ashamed to say that I was really looking forward to lunch and an early movie." She lowered her eyes. "Uh, well, I will admit that I was developing some deep feelings for our sweet Bob until several things didn't go his way, and he turned into a *really* scary person. Believe me, I was so frightened that I made an excuse and ran for my life."

Jealousy reared its ugly head. Nancy hissed, "He asked you to spend a whole afternoon with him? Why you?"

"Why not me?" Laura demanded.

"Ladies!" Josh pleaded. "Just stop it. It's obvious that the two of you have a crush on Bob."

"Make that past tense for me," Laura exclaimed. "I never want to see that evil face again!"

180

"Sorry," Nancy mumbled. "I still say you're wrong about Bob. But let's get back to the message that Marie is sending. If nothing can develop between the two of you, then what else could it be?"

Josh threw up his hands. "What other message could there be?"

Laura's voice was trembling when she answered. "What if…what if Marie wants you to protect me because I'm in danger?"

"Protect you from what?" Josh wanted to know.

Nancy waved her arms. "Why, protect her from the serial killer! Look at her, Josh. She's a blue-eyed blond with long legs! That's his specialty, and he's in the area, you know."

"He is? How do you know that?"

"You didn't hear how he tried to kill Joan at the Rehab Center?"

Josh shook his head.

Laura stepped into the conversation. "He dressed up like a woman and managed to get into her room. All this time, Joan hadn't said a word or reacted to any outside stimulus. If the killer had kept his mouth shut, Joan would be dead now. Recognizing his voice from her nightmares was enough to shock her out of her comatose state, and she woke up. Her screaming and scratching brought the guard back from wherever he was, but the killer got away."

"How awful! No, I didn't know that, but that means he's been living among us all this time. You'd think someone would have recognized him from all the wanted posters that are around town."

The three of them sat in silence, digesting the truth of Josh's statement.

Finally, Josh looked at Nancy and asked, "How did Bob end up living in your shack?"

Alarmed, she glared at him. "We were talking about the serial killer and you dare to bring up Bob's name again?"

"Humor me, Nancy."

"You are so wrong about him!"

"Nancy, please," Laura said softly, placing a hand on the woman's arm. Nancy huffed, shaking off Laura's hand and crossed her arms over her chest.

"Fine. I was raking leaves off our driveway the first time I saw him walking past my place. He didn't pay much attention to me that time, but later when he walked by again, he stopped to chat. He said he'd spent all his money on parts for his car and needed a place to stay until it got fixed. We agreed that he could live in the shack if he'd work for me with no pay."

"So, you really don't know anything about him. Right?"

Nancy sighed. "I was just glad to find someone to help me keep my business open."

"What we now know is that the garage that's fixing his car has to be within walking distance of your house. There can't be that many of them. I'll check that out today."

"But what about me?" Laura cried. "I moved to Nancy's place to be safe, but Bob lives here, too! If he really is as evil as Marie seems to think, do I want my children to be that close to him?"

Nancy huffed. "You're all being silly!"

Josh shook his head. "I don't think so." Remembering Bob's devil eyes, he made a quick decision. "Laura, how would you feel about living in my house? I built a fully equipped addition when Marie's mother came to live with us. It hasn't been used since her mother died last year."

"Are you sure about this, Josh? Aren't you going to get tired of the constant smell of perfume?"

"It's funny, but I don't smell it now. Wonder why?"

Laura shrugged. "Well, if you're sure…."

Nancy scowled. "So go, Laura. If you both think Bob is that dangerous, then go."

"Please, Nancy! Don't be upset. I really appreciate your offer but I believe it's best that I put some distance between Bob and me."

# Chapter 63

George was peering through the third hole he had drilled through the shack's wall when he saw the door to Laura's cabin open.

How sweet that she would be living close enough to give him time to win her back after his bad temper had messed up his Laura project. Having his subject fall in love with him was an essential part of the ritual. It was bad enough that he'd been forced to use such an unimaginative way in his attempt to do away with Joan. In fact, starting with setting her house on fire, nothing about the Joan project had gone right. If she had had a proper death, he'd be in another part of the country by now and not stuck here in a dark shack waiting for his beard to grow.

He was about to take his eye away from the newly-drilled hole when he saw that Nancy and her departing guests were carrying the suitcases and overnight bags that earlier had been taken into Laura's cabin. Some went into Laura's car, and the writer guy put the rest into his. Both of them said something to Nancy before they each went to their own car and drove away.

He felt naked when Nancy stood for a few moments staring at his shack before she turned and went back into her house. What was all that about? Had Laura moved out? When Nancy brought him his dinner, he'd ask her.

Time passed slowly in the dark shack as he counted the minutes until supper. By holding his watch up to one of the holes he could clearly read the numbers; Nancy would be knocking on his door, soon.

But the knock never came. Had she left his supper without knocking? He first looked out one of the holes to make sure no one was out there before he opened the door to check. There was no food. Puzzled, he waited for an hour, wondering what was going on. His curiosity and his empty stomach finally won; he was going to the big house no matter what. Hopefully, his beard had grown enough to cover his dimpled cheeks. With one last look out a hole to make sure it was safe, he grabbed some clean clothes, covered his bristly head with the ballcap, and left his shack. Breathing in the fresh air felt good after being cooped up in the cabin.

Using the key that Nancy had given him, he soon was standing in her foyer. In the distance, he could hear her voice. Maybe he could get in and out without her knowing he was in her house, but that wouldn't solve his hunger problem; he'd worry about that after he got cleaned up.

He almost made it to the bathroom when he heard her say his name. Why would Nancy be talking to someone about Bob Miller? He tiptoed past the fireplace to get closer.

"Yes, Sargent, that's what I said, the Gentleman Serial Killer." He could see that she was talking on the phone. "Are you listening? I have reason to believe he's working for me. My name is…"

Those were her last words before the fireplace poker silenced her.

With the poker still in his hand, George looked down at Nancy's bloody head with utter disgust. Shit. This was not supposed to happen. With the toe of his boot, he nudged her body, and when she didn't respond, he bent down and gingerly felt for a pulse in her bloody neck. Nothing. Now what? When another growl from his stomach reminded him just how famished he was, all thoughts of cleaning up the mess and getting rid of her body fled. On his way to the kitchen, he returned the poker to its stand by the fireplace, fully intending to clean it up and get rid of Nancy when his stomach was satisfied.


Fortunately for George, Nancy's house bordered a heavily wooded area. Grunting, he carried her out the back door and into the deep growth. Far from the house, he spotted a gnarly old tree with roots extending above the ground where disturbed dirt would be easy to overlook. Nancy was a small woman, but by the time he'd dug a shallow grave and dumped her body into it, he was exhausted. With the edge of his shovel, he smoothed over the top, and after a brief search, selected a rather large rock to hide the disturbed dirt. It amused him that the stone was harder to carry than Nancy.

184

While he was digging, he'd had time to think. When it happened, he was sure it was the end of everything. Where could he go to hide? How would he support himself in a strange place? Unless he figured something out, he was going back to prison. And then it hit. He didn't have to go anywhere…except move from the shack to the big house! He'd just say that Nancy had gone to take care of her sick mother and had put him in charge of the bed and breakfast. A "No Vacancy" sign would keep customers away, and the best part? He had the house all to himself, the better place to be when it was time to make Laura his.

He loved it when all his plans came together.

# Chapter 64

Laura and the two children easily settled into Josh's in-law suite, and as he'd promised, the addition offered complete privacy. All she ever heard from his part of the house was the clicking of computer keys when she was in the shared hallway.

Her sister had chosen well. Laura sighed over the picture albums Josh had made available, especially the wedding album. Marie and Josh's marriage had been a true love affair. It was hard to think that her sister had spent summers on the lake and yet they had never run into each other. If they had, would they have felt a connection? Which one of them looked like their mother? Marie had dark hair, so from which parent had she inherited that?

Knowing she would never find the answers to any of her questions, she laid down the album and looked at the time. If she put something in Marie's crockpot, she could go about her business while dinner cooked. When she borrowed it, she promised Josh there would be enough food for his dinner, too.

Leaving Nancy so abruptly was making her uneasy. They had been friends for years, and clearly she'd been upset with the way things had ended. Laura thought hard, but she couldn't remember if she had thanked Nancy enough for worrying about her safety. The least she could do was drive over there and apologize, hopefully without running into Bob. Even if she stopped to visit Joan on the way, she would still be on time to pick the kids up from school.

Joan was sitting on a chair when Laura stepped into her room. "Looking good, girlfriend!" Laura exclaimed, hugging her.

Joan had gone under the plastic surgeon's knife several times, and while it was still in its early stage, there were signs of improvement in her appearance. Skin grafts from her stomach were covering the name carved into her forehead, and new nails were growing. There were other parts of her body that George Knox had disfigured, but Joan hadn't shared those injuries with Laura.

"How are you doing?" Laura asked.

Joan made a face. "My forehead might look better, but you should see my stomach! The damn surgeon skinned me, and the stitches itch!" She made a scratching movement without touching herself.

"Ouch!" Laura sympathized. "Are you still having trouble sleeping?

Joan shuddered. "It's those horrible nightmares! I'd be so much better if I could forget my last encounter with that monster!"

"They keep you from falling asleep?"

"Oh, I fall asleep quite easily, but then his…his face," she paused to shudder. "A close-up view of his face jars me and I wake up screaming!"

"How awful! You did tell me that he was quite handsome. I've seen the wanted pictures, but that probably isn't exactly how he looks in person."

"Ha! Pretty is as pretty does, and I think he's hideous! Laura, did you ever notice that in all those pictures, there's not one of him smiling?"

"Can't say that I have."

With a smug look on her face, Joan exclaimed, "Well, take my word for it, there aren't any, and I know why that is!"

"There's a reason he's not smiling? And you know it?"

"Yes! He's a vain man, and he knows that the only thing that isn't perfect about his looks is his smile. One of his front teeth is chipped."

A cold chill swept over Laura, her eyes widened, and her heart pounded. How could she have once thought that Bob's chipped front tooth was endearing? Josh had been right; the killer had been living among them.

She had to warn Nancy. Grabbing her phone, she punched in numbers. "Nancy, Nancy! Pick up! Please pick up!" she yelled. And then the light on the phone disappeared. "Darn it all! My phone just died."

"Laura! What the hell is going on?" Joan jumped out of her chair. "What has gotten into you?"

Laura cried, "I've got to warn Nancy! That Bob Miller I've been telling you about? Remember it was right after you arrived at the hospital and I was trying to get you to respond? I told you I had seen a stranger in town. You reacted. Do you remember that?"

"I do. But you described a bald-headed man with a beard, and that wasn't what I wanted to hear. George Knox has a great head of black hair and no beard."

"What I left out of the description was the fact that the stranger had a chipped front tooth. If I had told you that, would it have made a difference?"

Joan gasped. "You think the stranger was George Knox?"

"I'm sure of it! That man now calls himself Bob Miller." Laura shivered. "I can't believe that George Knox never left the area; he just changed his appearance."

Joan nodded. "Yes, if you had told me about the stranger's chipped tooth, it would have made a difference. Looks like he just shaved his head and grew a beard!" Joan's face took on a pensive look. "I'm curious. Did he ever ask you to wear your hair a certain way?"

"No, he never…oh, wait a minute. Once when we were waiting for a table at the Omelet Shop, he gathered my hair in his hand and piled it on top of my head. He told me that he really liked the way I looked with my hair like that. But why do you ask?"

"The police know that his victims were all tall blue-eyed blonds, but I found out the painful way that there was another requirement." Touching the back of her head with both hands, she grimaced. "All his victims had to wear their hair in an upsweep. There's no way for the police to know that about him."

"Did he do that to you?"

Joan nodded. "He pulled handfuls of hair out of my scalp when he did it." She stopped to grab her friend in a fierce hug. "Thank God you were too busy rescuing me from my burning house to notice my hair."

Laura was returning the hug when she suddenly remembered the feel of the killer's arm around her shoulders, his soft kiss on her cheek, the lunch, and the aborted afternoon invitation. She covered her face with her hands, and cried, "Oh, Joan, I'm George's next victim!"

"No, no, no! Why are you saying that?"

Laura was trembling. "I always knew that I fit the tall blond description of his victims, but that hair thing!"

"That could be a coincidence. Anyhow, you aren't in love with him, and that's another one of his requirements."

"Joan, I *was* falling in love with him! How could I not love a man who was funny, exciting, considerate, religious…" She stopped when Joan's mouth dropped open.

"Religious?"

"Yes, religious. He can quote the Bible verbatim, and I even saw him pray for a woman at the Rehab Center. She got out of her wheelchair and walked."

"No! George Knox is the devil incarnate! We must be talking about two different men."

"What if I told you that he was paying a lot of attention to me? That we had lunches together and had movie plans? That he kissed me on the cheek?"

"Oh, Laura! Making his victim fall in love with him is what he does. He complained that he wasn't getting the usual satisfaction out of torturing me because I wasn't in love with him."

Laura swallowed the bile that was threatening to gag her. "It's him. I know Bob Miller is George Knox."

Joan smirked. "I'd love to see the look in his icy blue eyes when they confront him."

"Icy blue eyes?"

"Yes. Laura, what's wrong?"

Feeling as if someone had punched her in the stomach, she replied quietly, "Bob Miller has brown eyes."

"Come on, Laura! You know that doesn't mean anything!" Joan snorted. "You're forgetting that at the end of our college senior year, I changed the color of my eyes because the guy I wanted to date wrote in the yearbook that green eyes turned him on?"

"I'd forgotten about that! But now I do remember the trouble you had getting the contacts out of your eyes!"

"They stuck to my eyes like they were super glued!" Joan recalled. "Remember the night when I just couldn't get them out? I was crying, and some girls returning from a religious club meeting stopped in and organized a prayer circle?"

"Yes," Laura laughed. "And that was the last of the green contacts."

"Now that I've made the point that the color of eyes can easily be changed, do you really think this Bob of yours is George Knox?"

Laura nodded. "And please don't call him 'my Bob.' I admit I had a crush on him, but the other day I ran for my life when I saw the scary side of him."

"George Knox can be very charming...before he turns vicious." She pointed to her forehead. "Where is Bob now?"

"He's been living in Nancy's shack and doing handy work for her. She has a crush on him, too."

"Why do you think she's in danger? Nancy is a short brunette."

Laura didn't answer. Instead she asked, "How far is it to a police station?"

"Well, fortunately the police station is on the next block. I'm glad your phone isn't working because news this important should be delivered in person, so go be a big hero! I do believe there's a huge reward if your information results in his capture! Just think of the wild parties we could throw with all that money!"

Laura beamed; her old friend was back.

"Wish me luck!" Laura yelled over her shoulder as she ran out of Joan's room.

# Chapter 65

George pushed away from the table, drank deeply from a bottle of very expensive wine, rubbed his full stomach, and burped. He didn't bother to cover his mouth or excuse himself because the "No Vacancy" sign worked; he was the sole occupant of the big house. The food might have been better if Nancy had cooked it, but Nancy wasn't cooking anymore. It was only for a brief moment that he allowed himself a drop of remorse for killing her, but only a drop; she'd brought it on herself.

It had taken only two trips from his shack to transfer his meager possessions and the torture instruments to the big house.

He couldn't believe his luck. The house was loaded! A huge freezer had enough food for Nancy to feed her lodgers for weeks. Mike's closet was full of clothes and shoes, and his dresser drawers were stuffed with underwear, socks, and t-shirts. Even though he'd been dead for over a year, Nancy hadn't gotten rid of anything that he owned.

Euphoria gradually faded when reality hit, and it hit hard. His story that Nancy was out of town taking care of a sick mother would work for a limited time, and then what? Back on the run? Joan had handed him a gift when she'd crawled into the floral van and invited him into her house, a house that he later set on fire. And then Nancy had handed him another gift when she allowed him to stay in the shack and work for her. How many gifts were out there just waiting to be bestowed upon him? He was smart enough to know that the gift-giving-well had dried up.

The realization brought him back to the truth. If he were going to shut up the demons that were clamoring to be satisfied, he had to make a move on Laura right now before Nancy's many friends started to get curious. If he did it right, no one would suspect that he'd had anything to do with her disappearance. Hell, he'd even help look for her, and he'd cry with her friends. He just knew one thing; whatever happened, he was never going back to prison.

The tour of the house took him to the basement, and the thought of what he was going to do to Laura down here was making him giddy. It was going to be so satisfying!

He was familiar with old basements because his grandparents had lived in an old farmhouse, and his mother used to take him along when she visited them. Sometimes his cousins were visiting too, and playing hide and seek with them was always fun. Suddenly, in the middle of a pleasant thought, a strong feeling of anxiety swept over him, leaving him breathless. With a shake of his head he cleared his mind.

The entrance to his grandparents' basement was outside with a double-door-like contraption covering the opening. There was always one cousin who was big enough to open the two-sided door, giving them access to the whole basement to hide in. He was grinning at a memory of one cousin who, after a game of hide-and-seek, hadn't shown up for dinner. A panicky search for the kid found him sound asleep behind the furnace. He was still chuckling about the incident when another memory jolted him, leaving him breathless, scared and shaking. Whoa! Whatever it was, the substance of the memory disappeared before he could grab it. Wiping the sweat that had appeared suddenly on his forehead, he pushed the sensation away and continued exploring.

Something in the very back caught his attention. Spiders had woven their webs that stretched from the knob of a dusty door up to the ceiling, making it obvious that the door hadn't been opened in years. He paused for a while, trying to decide if seeing what was behind the door was worth tangling with the spiders. He hated spiders! Curiosity was stronger than his aversion, but not strong enough to stifle his scream that echoed in the basement when a big fat one landed on his arm.

When he finally calmed down, he stepped over the spider's squashed body and opened the door. The earthy smell of rich soil hit his nose. A root cellar! He knew all about root cellars because his grandparents had one. The cellar was a cave-like room that had been dug into the ground to escape the heat and cold on the surface. In those days, surviving the long winter months was hard unless you had a way of preserving the summer's harvest. He remembered helping his grandpa pick potatoes out of the dirt that one of his machines had unearthed. Those, along with onions, apples, cabbages, and turnips ended up in the root cellar.

What a find! Oh, this was going to be so good! An almost soundproof place to keep Laura! And when he killed her, he could dig a hole and bury her right here. He chuckled as he carried the shovel and the other instruments into the cave. Everything was going so right! Another gift?

Over the years, he'd used many kinds of torture, but they all had to do with physical pain. Depravation of sound and light would be mental pain, something new and different.

Like a kid with a new toy, he was excited. This was much better than his shack, even with its double layer of soundproofing material. He just had to try it out to get an idea of how the experience would affect Laura when he sealed her in. Gleefully, he stepped into the cellar and pulled the door closed…and saw his mother.

He couldn't breathe. Fear, terror, and panic paralyzed him. His mother was dead. Of that he was sure because he'd killed her. But here she was, with her blond hair piled high on top of her head and her long legs encased in black stockings, looking just the same as the day he'd shoved her into a shallow grave.

Memories buried so deeply that prison psychiatrists never unearthed came roaring back like a runaway freight train. He fell to the earthen floor of the pitch-black cellar screaming, "Mom! Don't lock me in! I promise! I'll be good! I won't do it again! Mom! Mom! Please don't lock me in!"

In the absolute silence of the dark cave, George lost consciousness.

# Chapter 66

The creepy feeling that George Knox was following her was strong enough to make her run to the police station. Breathing hard, she opened the door, sprinted into the station and slid to a stop at the front desk.

The uniformed man behind the desk stood up and greeted her. "That was quite an entrance! Someone chasing you?" he asked the beautiful blond who was still puffing from the short run.

Trying to catch her breath, she finally managed to say, "Could be."

Sergeant Gray raised his eyebrows. "Really?"

"Is there someone here I can talk to about George Knox, the serial killer?"

His eyes widened. "Are you the one who called the station about him before?"

Laura looked puzzled. "Someone else called about George? Did the caller give you her name?"

"No. She did mention the name Bob Miller along with George's but then the call ended abruptly, actually in the middle of a sentence."

"What did she say?"

"That was it."

"Nancy!" Laura blurted. "He has Nancy!"

"Who is Nancy, and who do you think has her?"

"Go!" Laura yelled. "Go before he does something hideous to her!"

"Go where?"

"The bed and breakfast owned by Nancy Blair on Main Street."

"I'm familiar with it. Now slow down and come with me to Captain Hetrick's office. He needs to hear about this."

"So when will you go check on Nancy?"

"When Captain Hetrick tells me to."

Laura was practically jumping up and down. "But you're wasting time! Nancy could be in real danger if he caught her calling the police!"

One tap on the door, and a voice muttered, "This better be important."

When Captain Hetrick finally opened the door, Laura pushed passed him with such force that he had to fight to maintain his balance. His mouth was open, ready to demand an apology, but when he came face to face with the hair-blown rosy-cheeked blond, all the air rushed out of his lungs, his tongue tangled with itself, and he couldn't think of a thing to say.

Sergeant Gray coughed into his hand trying to hide the grin that he couldn't hold back.

"Captain?"

"Uh, yes, Sergeant Gray. Will you excuse us?" he asked as he pulled the door closed, leaving the sergeant on the other side.

Sergeant Gray walked back to the front office silently fisting the air. After two years of celibacy following his wife's long but lost battle with cancer, the tall blond woman had broken through the wall. Captain Hetrick's reaction to the opposite sex had returned.

Inside the room, Laura studied the tall, dark and extremely handsome Captain Hetrick with a critical eye. Was he going to believe her story in time to save Nancy?

Holding out his hand he said, "Let me introduce myself. I'm Ralph Hetrick, the captain of this precinct. Please have a seat, and how may I help you?"

"We don't have time for niceties!" she cried, not taking his hand. "George Knox has been living among us! He's changed his appearance and calls himself Bob Miller. Nancy, the woman who runs the bed and breakfast on Main Street, has been allowing him to stay at her place for free while his supposed car is being fixed. In return, he helps Nancy run her business."

"And why do we need to rescue Nancy?"

"Because I think he heard her making the call to you."

"The call that informed us that the man on the wanted posters that are all over town is Bob Miller? We did some checking after that call, and found that the minister of one of the churches here in town just

195

can't say enough good things about Bob Miller. Seems Bob has caused an increase in church attendance, has a bible study group that has grown so large it can't meet in a private home anymore, visits patients at the Rehab Center to pray with them, and can quote the Bible verbatim. I'm sorry, Miss…I didn't catch your name."

Laura was pacing the room. "Listen! Bob prayed with the patients at the Rehab Center because he wanted to have access to Joan Wilberson. Remember what George Knox did to Joan? All his victims have to die, and because he set her house on fire, he never got to finish the ritual."

"Of course I remember Joan. We're working on that case, but the guard is still insisting that it was a woman that he chased away from her room."

"It was not a woman! It was George Knox! Joan heard his voice, and it shocked her out of a comatose state! Why are you sitting there, doing nothing?"

"I think you should sit down, take a deep breath, and let us do our job," Captain Hetrick said in a calm voice.

"Well, then do your job! You've got to grab this guy before he takes off!"

"What was your name again? Either I never heard it, or I just don't remember it."

"My name doesn't matter! Anyhow, if you don't catch him now, later you'll hear my name often enough."

He raised his eyebrow. "And why is that?"

"Because I'm his next victim!" Laura shouted.

There was a moment of silence. Captain Hetrick finally cleared his throat. "You realize that this is one wild story?"

"A story that's going to get wilder the longer you sit here and think about it," she grimly replied. "By the way, my name is Laura Baker."

"Uh, is that a Mrs. or a Miss?"

"I'm a widow," she answered in a flat voice.

She glanced at the clock on the wall and sucked in a deep breath. "Oh, my God!" she yelled. "My kids are home from school and I'm not there! And my car! It's back at the Rehab Center!"

Seeing a chance to spend time with the feisty Laura, Captain Hetrick exclaimed, "Tell you what Mrs. Baker, I'll take you home in a squad car, and then together we will all go and have a nice visit with Nancy Blair who I'm sure will be in good health when we find her."

Laura threw up her hands in dismay. "If this is the only way I can get you to rescue Nancy, fine. I guess it's better than nothing. But I sure hope I don't have to say, 'I told you so!' because if something bad has happened to Nancy, I will personally embroider those words on a pillow and make sure you put your head on it every night when you try to sleep."

# Chapter 67

George Knox opened his eyes and saw nothing but blackness. Was he blind? And then he remembered. Years of repressed memories thundered through his head, reducing him once again to a terrified boy whose pleas to his mother to let him out of the cellar went unheard. Just as he did then, he did now; he lost control of his bladder. Writhing on the dirt floor, he knew from his childhood experience that even though the warmth of the pee felt good initially, it soon would be just a cold wet spot that would later earn the wrath of his mother.

It wasn't until he'd worn himself out screaming, crying, and pleading that he was able to think rationally. His mother hadn't locked him in this time.

George pushed himself into a sitting position and felt around. He needed to find the front of the dirt cellar because that's where the door to freedom was located. It was a small enclosure, and as soon as he tripped over the torture instruments, he knew where he was.

With both hands extended, he felt around the wall, trying to locate a doorknob that, with one twist, would free him from this hellhole.

Where was the damn knob? He knew it was there because he'd used it to pull the door shut. He breathed a sigh of relief when his right hand encountered the cold knob. Already his mind was planning his next move of how he was going to entice Laura to the big house to check on her friend, Nancy. That should be easy enough to do, and he'd work on that plan as soon as he changed out of his cold wet pants that were sticking to his skin. With Mike's full closet, that wouldn't be a problem. Oh, he couldn't wait to hear Laura's screams and pleas when he introduced her to the exquisite terror of being locked up in the pitch-black root cellar. It was going to be delicious!

The sudden odor of perfume that filled the cellar was so strong, George was not only surprised, he was gagging. Where had that come from? When the intensity of the smell increased, he could feel the big meal he'd consumed churn unhappily in his stomach. Frantically, he turned the knob.

To his dismay, instead of opening the door to freedom, the knob came off in his hand.


Laura gathered her two scared children into her arms and cried with them. She didn't try to talk until their sobs subsided.

"Where were you, Mom?" Beth demanded.

"Yeah, Mom, where were you?" Teddy echoed.

"I'm so sorry!" Laura said softly. "It won't happen again, I promise!"

"We th..th..thought you left us like Daddy did!" Beth explained, and then the sobs started again.

Ralph Hetrick watched the little family drama with tears in his eyes. He and his wife had always planned on having a family.

"Mrs. Baker, isn't there a neighbor who would welcome your children if this should happen again?"

Laura's smile was rueful. "Myrtle Graham was the community's grandma around here. She welcomed any child who was locked out or left behind. Unfortunately, she fell and broke her hip and ended up in a senior living apartment. So, the answer to your question is no, there's no neighbor like that anymore."

"That puts a lot of pressure on you," he commented.

"There usually isn't a problem because I work at home."

He raised his eyebrows. "May I ask what your business is?"

"I'm an artist. Maybe you've seen my work in the window of A Touch of Color."

"That's you?"

Laura nodded.

An artist! Ralph smiled inwardly. The more he found out about this woman, the more he liked her. He'd admired the pictures in the store's window and had debated with himself. Did he really need another picture to put on his already crowded walls? Now that he'd met the delightful Laura, the indecision was over. He did indeed need another picture but not just any picture. His wall needed one of hers.

Her foot tapping in impatience, Laura turned to the captain. "We've got to leave right now! You might not think that Nancy is in danger, but I do!" Pointing to the car, she spoke to Beth and Teddy. "Kids, get in, and if you ask Captain Hetrick nicely, maybe he'll turn on the siren."

# Chapter 68

With the siren blowing, wide-eyed Beth and Teddy squealed with laughter as the squad car made its way to Nancy's street in record-breaking time. Even though the "No Vacancy" sign was on, there wasn't a car outside any of the cabins or in the main parking area.

"If all of Nancy's rooms are full, where are the cars?" Laura asked the captain.

"That is strange," he admitted. "'I'm going in and you and your children are going to remain in the car."

"Oh, no you don't!" Laura yelled. "I'm going in with you."

"And leave your kids out here, alone? I don't think so!"

Laura threw up her hands in defeat. There was no way she was going to leave her children unprotected in an area where a serial killer lived. "Okay, I agree. But if you go in and nothing seems to be wrong, I need to see for myself. I've known Nancy for a long time, and if something is different, I'll know it sooner than you will."

He nodded, and crawled out of the car. "If everything is fine, this shouldn't take long."

Laura sat in the car with Beth and Teddy and watched him approach the door. When no one answered his knock, he turned the knob, opened the door, and disappeared inside.

It seemed like forever, but it really was only a few minutes before he stuck his head out the door and motioned her to come in.

She hesitated. She really needed to go in, but she definitely couldn't leave her children alone in the car, and she definitely couldn't take them into a dangerous situation.

"Come on!" the captain yelled. "It's safe! There's no one in the house! It's empty."

"Come on, you two," she instructed her children. "Stay close to me and don't touch anything. If you behave yourselves, your reward is a stop at McDonald's on the way home."

Laura had to raise her voice above the kids' excited chatter to ask, "Everything okay?"

"Well, the house is empty, and that's what I was checking. Come on in and let's look around."

One look at the kitchen and Laura held up her hands. "Whoa!"

Heat from an open oven door was spilling into the room, the pans on the stove held food that was still lukewarm, and the coffee carafe was almost full.

"See, I told you Nancy is fine. She has to be around somewhere because the food on the stove is still warm."

Laura stood silently, surveying the carnage. Shaking her head, she flatly stated, "Nancy did not cook this meal."

"What?"

"Remember this is a bed and breakfast. Nancy had to cook for her boarders, so Nancy perfected the art of cleaning up as she cooked. I've had dish-duty after many of her meals, and really all there was to clean were the actual dishes and silverware because she'd washed the pots and pans after she transferred the cooked food onto a serving plate. Nancy didn't have anything to do with the cooking of this dinner."

"So then, who did?"

"You searched the house?"

"For people, yes. Let's walk through it and you tell me if you see anything out of place."

A half-hour later, they found themselves back in the kitchen.

"No Nancy and no George Knox," the captain stated. "There's no sign of a struggle, so I think your fears about the safety of your friend Nancy are ungrounded."

Laura wasn't listening. Where were her children? Had someone grabbed them when she wasn't looking? Frantically, she yelled, "Beth! Teddy? I told you to stay close to me! Where are you?"

There was no answer.

Her heart was pounding in her chest. If something had happened to her kids because she'd made the stupid decision to include them in this venture, she'd never forgive herself. Taking a deep breath, she yelled, "If you aren't in the kitchen by the count of three, there's no stopping at McDonald's on the way home. One, two…"

The sound of pounding feet coming toward the kitchen was music to her ears, but when that noise was replaced by the sound of a heated whispered argument, she yelled, "Get in here!"

With guilt written on their faces, both of them entered the kitchen with their heads down. Laura glared at them. "I gave you two orders. You were to stay close to me, and you were not to touch anything. Since you didn't obey the first order, I rather suspect that you didn't obey the second one, either."

Teddy and Beth looked at each other.

"So, I'm right?"

All this time, Teddy had kept his hands behind his back.

"You hiding something, Teddy?" Laura's voice was harsh.

Beth nudged him. "You have to show them!"

Slowly, Teddy brought his hands forward and held them out. They had blood on them.

Horrified, Laura cried, "Teddy, are you hurt?"

Beth piped in. "Mom, that's not his blood. It's someone else's."

Captain Hetrick stepped in. "Son, what did you touch? You can tell me, and I promise I won't yell at you. What your mother does to you when you get home is another matter."

"The poker," Teddy mumbled.

"The fire poker?" Laura asked.

Teddy nodded.


It had taken the cadaver-smelling dogs no time at all to uncover Nancy's shallow grave. Laura, her eyes red from crying, glared at Captain Hetrick. "You wouldn't listen to me! Look what happened! I told you so! I told you…" Laura sobbed.

Ralph Hetrick knew at that moment that any romantic hopes he'd had for a relationship with the lovely Laura were shattered.

# Chapter 69

Josh Lang reread his finished book. He was quite pleased with how it had turned out but in his review, he realized he hadn't fully described the shack back at Nancy's bed and breakfast. To strengthen the horrible events that followed, he needed to define it more in sinister detail.

When his fingers couldn't find the words to type his thoughts, he realized that he needed to go there and see for himself.

As he got closer to the bed and breakfast, he passed several squad cars that were leaving the area. An accident? Even before he pulled into the parking lot, he was puzzled by the lit "No Vacancy" sign, because the only car in the lot was a squad car. Yellow crime-scene tape that was fluttering in the wind made him wonder if all those police cars that had passed him had been coming from this house. Should he turn around and leave?

And then the smell of rotting flesh hit. Gagging, he opened his car door and jumped out, only to realize the odor was even stronger outside the car, and as he approached the house, it seemed to increase in intensity. With his nose buried in the crook of his arm, he rang the doorbell. When no one answered, he pushed the door open and went in.

The first thing he saw was Laura poking Ralph Hetrick in the chest, her face intent upon whatever subject it was that had her so worked up. He rather felt sorry for his old friend because he and the captain had both lost their wives around the same time, and one night after a few drinks at the local bar, they had actually cried together.

At first, they didn't acknowledge his presence. Either they hadn't seen him or maybe they just didn't want to end their argument, but it did end when Josh's muffled voice emerged from the crook of his arm where his nose was buried. "So, where is he?"

"Oh, hi, Josh! We didn't hear you come in. You missed all the excitement! The police just finished their investigation!"

Josh didn't even ask what investigation they were talking about. Instead his muffled voice was louder when he barked, "Where is he?"

"Who are you talking about, Josh?" Laura asked.

Josh uncovered his nose and gagged. "Bob Miller or George Knox. Pick one!"

Her forehead creased. "You can smell him? That's strange because he's not here. The sad news is that he killed Nancy before he left."

"Nancy is dead? Oh, no! That's awful! She and Marie were good friends. But why would he kill her? She doesn't fit the description of any of his victims."

"We think he caught Nancy calling the police telling them that she'd figured out that Bob Miller is George Knox."

"Bob or George, I don't care who he is, I just know that I smell this pungent odor when I get near the guy, and believe me, he's here!"

Ralph Hetrick looked puzzled. "You smell George Knox?"

"It's a long story," Laura told him. "I'll tell you, but not now."

The captain shook his head. "I'm sorry to disappoint you, Josh, but we've searched the house several times and so did the police who came with the cadaver dogs that found Nancy's grave. George Knox is long gone."

"Do you mind if I follow my nose?"

"Be our guest," Laura replied.

Walking behind Josh, who was taking turns sniffing and gagging, was Captain Hetrick; Laura and her children stayed in the kitchen.

"He really smells the guy?" the captain asked before following Josh to the basement.

"Yes he does, and he smells his wife's perfume when he sees me, but that's another story."

"Uh, Laura?"

"What?"

"Promise that after this is over, you'll explain it all to me?"

Remembering how hard she'd had to work to convince him that Nancy was in danger, she didn't answer immediately. Finally she reluctantly said, "Maybe."

Josh was gagging so hard he was having trouble walking. The basement was large, but once he got in front of the undiscovered door, he stopped. "He's in there." With that, he turned, ran up the stairs, almost knocking Laura down in his haste to find fresh air.

Captain Hetrick studied the door that everyone had missed. Was Josh right? George Knox was in there? Without backup, there was no way he was touching the door. A noise from behind the door made him freeze.

"Hello? Is anyone in there?" he yelled.

Muffled crazy laughter and animal-like sounds were the answer to his question. The hair stood up on the back of his neck. "Laura," he shouted. "I'm calling for backup! Grab your kids and get out of here! Go sit in my car and lock the doors! Oh, you'll need the keys!"

A quick search of his pockets didn't produce the keys. "I must have left them in the ignition," he yelled up to her. "But why would I do that? I never leave the keys in the ignition!"

"I doubt if anyone would steal a police car," Laura remarked. "Come on, you two. We need to get out of here before the backup team comes."

"Do we get McDonald's on the way home?" Beth asked.

Laura thought before she answered. "Maybe."

While she walked through Nancy's splendid house, she said a prayer for the woman who would never enjoy another day in it. If only the authorities had listened to her! But really, she had to admit that no one could have saved Nancy. He'd killed her in the middle of her call to the police station.

The squad car was still parked in front of the big house, and sure enough, she could see the keys dangling from the ignition. Surprised that a police captain would be so careless, she wasn't paying attention to her surroundings. It was Teddy who saw him first.

"Mom, there's a crazy man following us!"

Laura looked back over her shoulder, and what she saw terrified her. A wild-looking Bob Miller that she now knew was George Knox, was laughing and screaming obscenities as he headed for them.

"No!" she cried. Throwing her arms around her two children, she steeled herself for what was coming next, but George ran past them

206

as if they weren't there. She was still huddling with her children when the squad car roared to life, and with George Knox at the wheel, disappeared down the street.

Alarmed, Teddy asked, "Who was that, Mom?"

"A really bad man," she answered.

Had Captain Hetrick stupidly opened the door?

Two police cars raced down the street and slammed to a stop at the empty curb. The doors opened, and uniformed police rushed toward the house.

"Wait! Wait!" she yelled.

"Not now, lady," one of them yelled.

Grabbing her children's hands, she pulled them toward the house. "Hurry! We have to let them know that George has escaped."

By the time they entered the house, they could hear excited voices coming from the basement.

"To the basement!" she yelled.

Teddy broke away from her, ran down the steps and straight to the captain who was peering into an empty root cellar. "We saw him! That bad man stole your car, and now we can't go to McDonald's!"

Captain Hetrick whirled around, and seeing Laura, he demanded, "What is he talking about?"

"Teddy's right. George ran past us, jumped into your car, and drove off!"

"Men! To your cars! I'm calling the state police for backup. We need to find George Knox before he gets out of the area!"

Left alone, Laura stepped closer to the opened room that Captain Hetrick had called a root cellar. On the floor of what looked a cave, she could see hammers, a saw, nails, and pliers that were partially covered by the dirt from the big hole in the roof that was flooding the cave with daylight.

Standing alone was a shovel that, for some unknown reason, made Laura shiver.

# Chapter 70

"I'm not leaving!"

"Mrs. Baker, you and your children can't spend the night at the police station."

"Why not? Until I know that George Knox is back behind bars, I'm not going home."

Captain Hetrick sputtered. "B..b..but...."

"No buts about it! He knows where I live, he knows that I live alone with my children, he knows I have a garage to hide the stolen squad car...you know, the car you left the keys in?"

Ralph Hetrick's face burned. He knew why he'd done it but he couldn't admit it to her. How could he think of mundane things like keys when the beautiful and gutsy Laura was sitting beside him?

Laura continued. "Look. You have to know that no one can disappear as quickly as he did unless he found a way to hide the squad car. I suggest you check garages, and when you find one with the squad car in it, you will know that the people inside the house are either tied up or dead."

The captain replied in a soft and soothing voice. "I understand that you're scared, but...."

"Understand?" Laura shrieked. "Until he chooses you to be his next victim, you will never understand!"

Stepping back, he held up his hands. "Calm down! I said we would find a way to protect your family, and we will. But right now, we have another problem."

Laura's finger poked Ralph's chest with each word. "There will be no new discussion about anything until we solve my family's safety problem!"

"Roscoe."

"Roscoe? My dog?" Her finger quit poking. "How did he get into this conversation?"

"I figured that would get your attention! Your neighbor called. Seems Roscoe is barking quite frantically."

Her forehead creased. "That's odd. Roscoe hardly ever barks."

"That's probably why they are calling. Oh, maybe he has to go out?"

Laura looked at the time. "No, he's good for a few more hours. It's close to his feeding time, but that wouldn't make him bark."

"We just got another call, so why don't I drive you home...." He stopped in mid-sentence because Laura was jumping up and down.

"He's there! George Knox is in my house! That's why Roscoe is barking!"


Captain Hetrick and his men came to a sudden stop outside the walk-in closet in Laura's bedroom. Roscoe, his muzzle red with blood, was frantically scratching on the closet door while a hysterical voice from inside was trying to reason with him.

"Is that blood on my dog's face?" Laura cried. "Is he hurt?"

Ralph whirled around. "I told you to stay in the car!"

"It's my house and my dog! I have every right to be here!"

"Even if the guy in your closet is George Knox?"

"Ha! Wonder if he has any favorite Bible verses to quote about his present situation," Laura hissed. Roscoe barked again, drawing her attention. "Pease tell me it's not Roscoe's."

"Pretty sure it belongs to the guy in the closet."

"Roscoe bit him? My dog doesn't bite!"

"I guess Roscoe did what he had to do, and thank God that he did!"

"What's this?" Laura pointed to a pair of men's pants and jockey shorts on the floor.

When Ralph reached down and picked them up, a strong smell of ammonia hit their noses. Laura had changed enough diapers to recognize the odor.

"Well, well," she commented. "Whoever is in the closet has peed his pants."

"Do you have any of your deceased husband's clothes in that closet? He's probably in there looking for dry pants."

"No. Goodwill got everything."

"This is going to be interesting," the captain snorted. "The guy has no pants on!"

"Ugh!" Laura wrinkled her nose. "How about a pair of my pink panties? That's the only thing I have that might cover him a bit."

"If that's it, then give me a pair and then you leave the room."


It was a wild looking George Knox who was screaming threats and obscenities as the police dragged him out of Laura's house. His bald head was covered with spiked new growth, his beard was sparse, his hands were handcuffed, and his feet were shackled. The red blood from Roscoe's bites that was running down his bare leg clashed with the pink of the stretched-to-the-limit panties that almost but not quite covered him. His one moment of sanity was when he saw Laura. All screaming threats and obscenities stopped as his icy blue eyes connected with hers. Separately, he mouthed the words, "We. Are. Not. Finished."

# Chapter 71

Laura's eyes looked up at the handsome face of the gentleman who was seating her at an outside table at The Hatch. When Ralph Hetrick bent down, placed his hands on her cheeks and lightly swiped his lips over hers, her memory flashed back to that day when she'd watched her late husband do exactly the same thing to Joan. The difference was in the type of kiss; Ben's kiss had been passionate while Ralph's was brotherly. However, the look on Ralph's face was not the least bit brotherly.

It had been months since Roscoe's role in the capture of the Gentleman Serial Killer had made headlines all over the country. For a few days, the political news had taken a back seat to the picture of the mutt with the blood-covered jaws. The novelty of a dog catching the bad guy had died down and life was now back to normal.

During that time, Ralph had courted Laura with flowers, chocolates, and a singing group that sang a love song under her bedroom window. Even though she knew that Ralph probably never had a chance to save Nancy, she didn't accept his dinner invitation while she mourned the loss of her friend.

Joan, whose intense sessions with Dr. Zumwalt had helped bring closure to her traumatic encounter with the serial killer, was always there when she needed support. Laura chuckled just thinking how Joan's life was soon going to drastically change; she and John were adopting soon-to-be-born twins. John never found out about the desperate things Joan had done while trying to find a successful sperm donor, and Joan never knew that John had aborted her fetus. Once again, just as in their childhood, Laura was the keeper of secrets.

The dinner tonight, according to Ralph, was for Laura to help him understand the unexplainable things that had occurred leading up to the capture of George Knox. Laura had trouble believing it herself, so if Ralph raised his eyebrows over what she was about to tell him, she wouldn't hold it against him.

It wasn't until after they'd placed their dessert order that Ralph finally leaned close to her and asked, "Now, when that writer guy said he could smell the killer, was he kidding?"

Laura set down her cup and looked around for the waitress with the coffee carafe. Why does it always seem that they're around when you don't want them, but when you do need them, they're nowhere to be found? On second thought, maybe what she needed was something stronger than coffee. Since neither choice was available, she pushed her cold coffee to the side, took a deep breath...and stopped when she suddenly realized that what she was about to tell was a love story. It had been Marie's love for her that had kept her alive and safe from the boogeyman.

The sound of Ralph clearing his throat interrupted her thoughts.

"Uh, Laura?"

Jerked back to reality, Laura tucked her new insight away to think about later. "Sorry about that."

When she noticed that the attentive expression on Ralph's face was so similar to what she saw every night at Beth and Teddy's story time, she just couldn't help herself.

Leaning across the table, she started the story in a breathy and mysterious voice. "Once upon a time...."

# Author Acknowledgements

Writing is a lonely and almost God-like occupation. The writer fills his imaginary world with living breathing characters who have names, attributes, and personalities. And then, like God, the writer has the power to choose which of them will succeed, which ones will have their heart's broken and which ones won't make it to the end of the story.

Writing might be a lonely occupation, but it's an exciting one.

The writing bug didn't bite me until I was well into retirement. But once it hit, it became an obsession. A day without writing, to me, is a day without sunshine. I had never written a short story, but once I started, I couldn't stop. The first venture into my new interest was writing six books in The Accidental Mystery Series, followed by a two-book series, *The Coat* and *The Collar*, then *Sweet Adeline,* and now *Essence.*

I have a circle of friends who not only are very supportive, they also keep my feet planted firmly on the ground with their sharp red correcting pencils. Every time I tell them I've written yet another book, a few of them roll their eyes. I think I'm wearing them out.

In writing *Essence,* I sent sections as I finished them to Judy Freed and Pat Bell. The editor of Ink Smith, Corinne Anderson, worked her magic, and the story is much better because of her.

*Evelyn Allen Harper*

The daughter of a coal miner, Evelyn left the hills of Pennsylvania to attend Anderson College in Indiana (now Anderson University) and then to Michigan where she earned a Masters at Wayne State University.

Evelyn lives with her husband, Barry, in a home they built on the shores of lovely Pearl Lake near Empire, Michigan.

Visit Evelyn online at www.evelynallenharper.com!